IMPRINT

WILDCAT SCREAMING

a novel by MUDROOROO

NAROC

🏛 Angus&Robertson
An imprint of HarperCollins*Publishers*

An Angus & Robertson Publication

Angus&Robertson, an imprint of
HarperCollins*Publishers*
25 Ryde Road, Pymble, Sydney, NSW 2073, Australia
31 View Road, Glenfield, Auckland 10, New Zealand
10 East 53rd Street, New York NY 10022, USA

First published in Australia in 1992
Reprinted in 1993

National Library of Australia
Cataloguing-in-Publication data:

Nyoongah, Mudrooroo, 1938– .
    Wildcat screaming.
    ISBN 0 207 17712 0.
    I. Title.
A823.3

Cover illustration by Gretta Kool
Typeset in 11/12pt Berner Australia by Midland Typesetters, Victoria
Printed in Australia by Griffin Paperbacks, Adelaide

9 8 7 6 5 4 3 2
97 96 95 94 93

To the men who did time in Fremantle Prison

WOUNDED IN ACTION

1

Back Again

Well, I can dream can't I? Dream?—nightmares, more like it. All I have to do is dream, dream, scream . . . I'm now walking through this posh suburb, walking?—more like slinking. Wildcat on the prowl. Naw, though maybe checking out the streets for a bust. Eyes dart this way, that way, all ways, focus, man, on the main chance. Take it and break it real good; but are there any chances left? Not with my luck! Yeah, it's like that! And then this kid, this tiny kid with mum in tow oozing milk outa her breasts so that I can smell it and all anxious loving eyes, but not for me, comes outa this nice neat home and across the nice neat closely cropped green lawn, smooth as a snooker table. And they come onto the nice clean pavement, littered only with this slinking black cat, who has no business being there except to raid their neat rubbish bins with their garbage all wrapped up and sprayed so that it'll smell good as that woman oozing her milky smell, though not for me.

The kid catches her distaste, she ain't ever going to give me a saucer full, and picks up a pebble and with all the viciousness that kids are capable of, flings it at me. It hits me on the right leg, shinbone, and I look down at the instantly formed scar, still hurting like her glance, like her milky smell, and I stare at that kid with murder in my eyes, and snarl: 'You rotten little brat, just wait till I get hold of you.' I drag my leg towards him and the white lady, the mum becomes all hot and bothered, she flushes red. 'You gotta have protection in this world,' I begin; but she isn't listening.

Her milky smell turns sour; her eyes incandescent with morality turn, spitting fire and fury at me. 'He's only a child,' she says.

'Ain't we all, lady, and I'm going to get that fucker . . .' and just then the leg collapses under me and I'm down on my hands and knees, belly down flat on the ground, ears laid back and tail droopy. Just a pussy cat. Nice looking one though, but she won't take me in; not even a sour saucer of milk for me. Another stone lands on my back and I scoot away. The lady laughs and says: 'You aren't no child, you're just an animal and should be locked up . . .'

Well lady, you've got your wish. This so-called menace to society is not going to slink around your nice clean lives for a long, long spell. They're, you're going to lock him up . . .

So much for dreams and nightmares, screams and accusations. Now I'm suffering just for being alive and not doing so well outa it. Just sitting here with my arm hurting like blazes and my mind hurting like blazes, and there's a scream sounding and resounding in my head. Shake it, sound tremolos, screeches to a new height, cuts out. Blessed silence; but, man, I'm more than depressed. Depression you can wear, dig? But this is more than that. Like all those sad songs you bought from the jukebox ganging up on you and dragging at your guts. That's how I'm feeling. Got the 'Who's Sorry Now Blues', and I'm huddling there filled with all that painful feeling, when this old digger with the scabby face, you know, the old red and peeling one of a true rummy, enters my misery and goes into this spiel. Yeah, man. I listen, got to get my mind off my troubles, off the misery in my guts, off the pain from that arm. The right one, because the cops in their infinite wisdom forgot that I was left-handed when they broke it. Stupid cunstables!

'I was at the Cove,' says the old codger. '9th Battalion, 1st Company under Red Ryder. Anzac Cove, went in on the first boat, and guess what?' he asks.

4

'Well, guess what?' I fling back at him.

'We hit the wrong bloody spot and get just this far up that bleeding beach. Red Ryder said "all over", but it was the wrong bloody beach and we get just this far over,' he replies, moving a space between his two trembling hands.

'Well, my great-grandfather was at the battle of Pinjarra,' I retort, not being provocative, but sorta to put him in his silly old place, though what battle was it when they came up on us, men, women and children and shot us down making us no tomorrow . . .

'Never heard of that one, mate,' he replies, his ears pricking up as if to appropriate it for later use; and I think would Jacko Turk understand this thing they done to us?

'Yeah, it's when you blokes murdered a lot of us Nyoongahs, men, women and children,' and I smile (if looks could kill) at him as he switches off like a good soldier hearing the word 'volunteer'.

'I was at the Cove,' he begins again, and I can't help thinking that he's evading the issue of my smile. He repeats again, adding detail for my delectation. 'I was at the Cove,' he repeats adding detail as if it meant something to me. 'I was at the Cove,' he repeats, as if it'll mean more to me by repetition. 'Ever been in a big mob of ships?' He goes on, 'Ever been amongst a big mob of men waiting and thinking while they order you here and there and back again? It was like that, nice peaceful night with the orders shouting up at the starry sky and they push us into those boats. Thirty or forty to a boat, squashed in like sardines, mashed together like bully beef. Little steam boat come puffing up, lines are thrown, linking us up, three boats to that little tug, and then we are off to God knows where. The land humps on the horizon, but as we are just out from Gyppoland we know it ain't France. We hang in there, not muttering a word 'cause we are ordered not to. Dark and peaceful, just before dawn. But, cobber, what I remember still is a bloody great flare coming out of the funnel of that tug. It scares the shit outa us, but you know, there is worse to come . . .'

5

'Worse to come,' I mutter. There is worse to come, yeah.

'Worse,' he repeats. 'Know what happens to poor diggers, like me? Discarded, like you Abos,' he whines. 'What use are we when the fighting's done? Cannon fodder, mate, that's us.'

'Well, you shouldn't go waving that gun of yours around,' I sneer, for he's a flasher as well as a rummy.

'But, you know what,' he goes on with that one-groove mind of his, 'can take this place standing on me head. Army life, cobber, army life is just like boob. What can they throw at you after you've had the sergeant major dressing you down, up, sideways and back, you tell me that?'

'Yeah, it'll be just like those good old days again, won't it? That sergeant major of yours is now a screw, ain't he?'

'Yeah, but he wasn't at the Cove,' the silly old bugger says, just as if the arm of the gramophone has been lifted up and the needle set at the beginning of the platter again. And I sit there letting him gas on. He's definitely not a 'gas', nor does he even begin to take my mind off my aching arm and woes.

You see I too have been at 'the Cove' so as to speak. With my rifle in my hand and all that shit. Another kid on the warpath and it's led me back again to here. Just a boy giving it all away at nineteen. Had a kiss and a feel at least. Gotta remember that, for it'll be all I'm having for a long, long spell. Man, I'm buggered. Buggered myself, but you tell me, what I was supposed to do? Join the army and fight in Korea, then come back and be just like this silly old sod? What's the use? My arm's hurting, okay; and I'm feeling sorry for myself, well okay, all right! See, I'm in this courthouse cell, just waiting to be sentenced and it's got to be a long one. They going to throw away the key, mate, I shot a copper, and you just don't do that in West Aussie or any other state of the Federation. They don't like it, witness my broken arm. They done that after the kicking I got. This big copper takes out his baton real slow and real deliberately. He stands there rubbing his hand slowly up its length as if it was his prick, though it's black and hard, not white and flabby like his'un. Then he lifts it and strikes out at my head. I raise my arm and bingo, my arm falls by itself.

'Jesus, you've broken his arm, Mick,' the copper who's just put in the boot says.

'Meant it to be his flaming head,' the cunstable retorts. His arm coming back for another blow, then stopping in mid-air, since he can't do two things at the same time, and he's still talking. 'Black bastards like him's gotta be taught a lesson.'

Well, all this time, I'm huddled there quaking and shaking and then the blow comes and I fly out like a light to a place where those coppers can't follow me. Hospital for a couple of days sure done me the world of good. They could've killed me those bastards, and all because I nicked one on the arm. Rotten shot that. Perhaps I should've got into the army and learnt to shoot straight. Naw, with my rotten luck, I'd be minus a leg or an arm now . . .

'Jacko Turk . . . well, it was bayonet to bayonet. The cold steel, cobber . . .'

'And the cold chill, bloke,' I answer, listening on as he details his exploits on the field of honour, then switching off to flashback on my own particular exploit, which should've come off. It should have; but this cat ain't got any luck but foul.

It was after that rage rising from being with those snotty University bods and not digging it one bit, that I flashed along the sweet beckoning light towards my particular den of crime, or as the magistrate described it when I was young enough to go before a magistrate and not the hanging judge: 'a bleeding ground of crime'. They have a way with words, don't they? I couldn't resist changing that adjective. It sounds better. We are the bleeding ground of crime. So I float in there, and meet this mate, who later only got a year for the bust and the car, while they wait, are waiting to launch the big one at the copper-shooter-upper—me!

Well, I'm getting a little ahead of myself, though still in the past. Let's get back to floating along that light beam. Wildcat with his eyes dazzled by the light while thoughts flash into his brain. I decide that the state has nothing to offer me, and that my chances, whatever they might be, will be better served in the east. Big place that. The mystic east of Sydney and Melbourne where the lights are always beaming out a welcome to me. Blokes tell me the trains stay only a second at the station and if you don't leap on, you get left behind like a stupid hick, and those trains are electric and in Sydney they got a subway. Wow, man! But to get there I have to get together the necessary cash, and where else to plan to get some than in that bleeding ground of crime. So natter to my mate and the upcome is we nick this car and zoom off into the night with the radio blaring out some of that young rock'n'roll, the blacker the better. Little Richard, Fats Domino, Tee-Bone Walker, the great Chuck Willis. My kinda music. Rebel music. Revenge music, sounding loud though not often on the radio in this stolen car whizzing me back to my home town to get loot for the mythical east. Christ, gotta get my grammar right, maybe. I'm in boob and all those long hours in your cell go quicker if you have your face in a book. Even read *The Modern World Encyclopedia*, 1935 edition. Real up to date. Look up Australia and us mob. Man, it gives you something to be depressed about. Cold bloody bastards these white blokes. 'Aboriginal Race. The survivors of the primitive inhabitants are found chiefly in the N. and do not exceed 60,000 in number; they are a declining race. Like the flora and fauna, they represent an archaic survival; they are perhaps related to the ancient Malayo-Indonesian race: they are dark brown in colour, with black wavy hair and a retreating forehead . . .'

So it goes on like that, and guess what I've got dark wavy hair, though I'm just brown because a white bloke got his wick in somewhere along the line. And you notice that they don't tell you anything about why us'uns are declining and surviving. Well, my great-grandfather was at the battle of Pinjarra and he survived that along with just a few others. And here I am too surviving just with this aching arm and this old digger telling how he's been surviving in the First World War. Silly old prick!

'Well, Cap'n Red Ryder, he takes one look at that cove and shouts: "Christ, they landed us in the bloody wrong place. Come on, lads, come on." Not a shot comes at us as we fix bayonets and charge across the beach and to a rise. We reach it and that's when the bullets begin. They go "peep-peep" as we charge through the scrub and blunder along. We hope the Cap'n knows where he's going, for sure as hell we don't . . .'

'Amen, mate,' I break in, 'guess it's better here. At least we know where we're bound for.' You can't stop the record once it's started, and he ignores my comment and I fall back into my thoughts and seek to find the place where I'm at. I don't work like a book. My mind's here, there and right now back in my little home town, that's if us Nyoongahs have a home town. Well, just say that I was raised there. Yes, I was and had a mum and sisters and brothers for part of the time, a few uncles, but never can recall any dad. Well, that's how things are. Now, let's get on with the story. Let it flow easy, let it flow slow, huh, Wildcat do your strutting.

We cruise into town, down that main street real slow, taking it easy, and pull up in a side street near the store I hold in my mind. Now it's here. Action! There's a yard behind filled with petrol and oil drums. Over the gate we go. This town is quiet; this town lies down like a sleeping dog; this town is deadsville. Not even a ghost moves. Not a dog whines. But Wildcat is on the hunt. We make some noise getting into the store. Real dark inside. Flash a torch around. Fuck, the beam hits a window. No worries, this town is a cemetery and the dead don't walk. It's then, I select me a nifty rifle. Always wanted to own one, and now I got one. Bullets too. But just for show, you dig, I don't think of shooting anyone. Killing people is only legal in the army, buddy, and in the movies. Gangster movies I like. James Cagney, Little Caesar, tough and mean, but cool. Poor bloody Indians though in those Westerns. Never saw them win, not even once. Thousands of battles of Pinjarras, and all in glorious technicolour. That's how it is for us'uns, that's how it is. Try to make a stand and they shoot you dead.

Still, like Little Caesar I load that gun, then get the loot, enough to get us east. Outa that store and back into the yard. Discovery. Yup, just like Australia's been discovered. Someone alive after all in this graveyard. The dead walk. Duck down behind a pile of drums just as this powerful beam of light hits me in the face. Bang; off and running. That's how I shot the cop. Big deal huh? Not much motivation there. Accident or what, I receive the big payback later for it. In bruises and this broken arm. Puts me in hospital, thank God, away from their grateful hands and boots. And now I'm waiting to be sentenced, locked in a cell with the old digger who's just pulling outa the Dardanelles and into this cell along with me. Well, it's going to happen any minute and I'm feeling kid scared, Anzac scarred because I'm only nineteen and I've shot an enemy . . .

You know, in a past time, they take me away from my mum and put me in Cluny. I cry for three whole days and get over it, eventually. You know, there is the first time, they slam me in the slammer. I sorta shrink inside, but I get over it. You know, there is the time I get released, and as the gates swing open to let me through, I sorta feel my skin hardening all over. These are hard acts to follow, but I follow them up by shooting a cop, and now I've got all those nasty feelings in my guts again as I stand in that high dock staring over the courtroom. Why, I'm almost on the level of the judge. He glances at me with eyes that don't see me. I'm nothing to him, man, just some dirt to be swept away. Well, I don't wear a silly red gown and a stupid grey wig. Who does he think he is—the fairy godfather? He glances my way again and I can't help smirking at him. And he gets a mean look in his eye; but now I know that

I'm something to him, just as Jacko Turk became something to that old digger, Clarrie, who's just got six months. Lucky old fart!

I look down into the body of the court where funny wigs are bent over papers, and really, man, I don't wanta be at this fancy-dress party. I want out! But I won't get out. Their words flow over me; the judge stares at me as if I'm an enemy of the state, and declares that I'm a menace to society and that society must be protected from the likes of me. He goes on and on. I think back to the battle of Pinjarra and wonder if any judge said anything about that day when they murdered our men, women and kids in cold blood and my great-grandfather just a kid of nine, the same age as I am when I'm taken from my mum, sees his mum die. Guess we were all enemies of the state then too and have to be taken care of for the good of their society.

Well, I don't wanta be here and I wish he'll get the whole thing over. At last he stops with the patter and gives me a long, long look. I know he's going to get even for that smirk. I listen as he sentences me to ten years at the Governor's Pleasure, and it's then that the scream begins again in my mind. If I was holding that rifle now. If I am holding it now, maybe I'll turn it on myself, cut off that scream for ever. That's how I'm feeling, you dig?

The cop guides my body back down into the cell. The black van waits to take me and the muttering old digger, Clarrie, to Freeo. I don't know how to react. There's this screaming going on and on in my head, going on and on in my head blotching out all thought. I don't know what to do, man, don't know what to do, would you?

Wildcat's eyes sparkle as he listens to Crow. Crow opens his beak and gives gleeful squawks which bode no good for the wild cat. He brings out his claws and lifts a paw. 'Now you don't take on so,' Crow caws, giving a little jump backwards. 'No worries, you want to fly? Well, I'm telling you, giving you the proper info. Now, listen here. Dead secret this. Tonight the moon'll be full. Well, you put your eyes on that moon. Fasten them there and keep on looking and looking. Maybe, better that you climb a high tree. Less distractions up there, and closer to the moon too. Just look at him, keep on looking and you'll lift off, fly higher and higher towards that old moon.'

Wildcat nods trying to be wily. Crow gives that squawk again. He hops around the wild cat, seeming awful gleeful. 'And what you want in return?' Wildcat asks. 'You know, scratch my back and I scratch yours'—and he extends his claws and Crow's glee leaves him. He gets into a kind of panic, and his wings open and he flutters out of reach just above Wildcat on a low branch. Wildcat bears his fangs. Opens his mouth in a great big yawn, giving Crow a glimpse of his rippers and tearers. 'You're a tricky one,' he says. 'So just look at what you're up against.' So Wildcat snarls; but all the time in his mind is the image of Crow just lifting off the ground as if the sky belongs to him. He wants to do that, wants to fly far and free.

'Man, would I jive you?' Crow says in his hipster talk.

'Man, you would,' Wildcat says, very much the bodgie, very much the cool cat in his dark threads.

'Not this time,' Crow answers him, slow and easy to put him off the track. 'You eat and leave me a feed, that's all I ask. We work together after this. You flying will be able to catch anything on legs or wings. Just give me my share, that's all I ask.'

And Wildcat relaxes and begins to believe Crow. It won't hurt to try, and if Crow is lying, well, there won't be a crow to crow around much longer.

That night, the moon leaps up into the sky. Wildcat wary at first gazes at it from the ground. It begins to call him, singing a sweet sky song to him.

> Arrh arrh, munya mayeamah yah-arah,
> Fly up and touch my skin.

And Wildcat begins climbing this big old gum tree. His claws grip and he pushes himself up higher and higher, right to the very top, where he clings with his back paws and feels himself swaying, swaying, swaying and the moon calling, calling, calling to him. He leaps off and up, one foot, two foot, and begins falling, falling, falling, screaming, screaming, screaming . . .

'And we come to this cliff, cobber, about as high as a prison wall. There's a kind of a path up it and up we go with blokes dropping all around. All mates, not bloody pack rats, and we come out onto a flat bit of dirt, Pluggie's Plateau as big as an exercise yard, but it's as if the guards are lined up shooting down at you. A cobber, Tom, he gets two bullets in the left leg, another through his hat, another one through his sleeve and a last one that hits his ammunition pouch. I'm lucky, a bullet glances off his entrenching tool and gets me in the arm. There's the scar, mate, see it. Bloody shambles it was, bloody shambles, just like going through the gates of hell, cobber. Just like that. Blokes falling down everywhere, wounded screaming everywhere: the gates of hell.'

And I come outa my funk, come outa that screaming dive into the sound of that old digger's voice and through the barred windows of that van, I catch a glimpse of the outside walls of the prison. The van halts. I should've been looking out and storing up the memories of streets and cars. Instead I was inside myself and that scream. I've missed everything that should've mattered to me, and now the van has stopped outside the gates. They swing open and we enter through into my home for umpteen years . . .

Well, what else was I expecting. A holiday on Rottnest? Though that isn't a good place for Nyoongahs. One big prison. Devil's Island. Creepy place. The spirits of the oldies are roaming around there still trying to escape. Well, it's what I've heard. Don't make up things like that, or even

13

believe them for that matter. Still, I ain't been to Rottnest. Been to Freeo though. In there now, and perhaps worse things have happened here. Freeo, that's a pun. I read all these books and that encyclopedia and like to air my knowledge. Ain't got anything else to do with it, have I, you dig?

Well, back to the van, and the gates open and the engine starts and we lurch forwards to where they ain't going to welcome me with open arms. A week or so out and back for longer than I can bleeding imagine. I don't know, I don't know. I can't do it on my head. I'll flip out if I think about it.

They open the back door of the van and the old digger Clarrie is the first one out. His old serge major is waiting for him, and he, that's Clarrie, comes to attention and gives him a big salute. 'Come off it, you silly old sod,' the screw shouts. 'Your brains scrambled, or something. This ain't no bloody army camp. It's worse than that.'

All the same, the screw has put a grin on his big red mug; but he scowls when I get out. 'Well, well, who do we have here,' he shouts; but I notice he keeps his distance. It's then I start to realise that perhaps going after a copper means something here. It means you could go after one of them too, and something else. Coppers and screws hate each other. That means I won't be getting bashed up for doing one of them.

I line up with Clarrie and we are marched into reception. Well, I'm used to it. Ain't nothing new to this wild cat. It's the same old eye-fucking thing with the stripping off of everything that makes us what we are. Poor old Clarrie, the flasher is able to flash all he wants to. Feel a bit sorry for him. No one here wants to look at his old limp prick. All the same, I sneer, 'Flash it Clarrie!' Then ease off as he looks at me as if all his humanity has been lost. Well, what was his flashing but a sign of his humanity. He lost something at Gallipoli, and so became a rummy and flashed what he thought was his manhood at the world. Silly old cunt, okay; but does that make me a silly young fuck? Naw, never!

Still, he makes his stand just as I make my stand. Now that stand is taken away from us. We are naked bodies to be arse examined by a doctor, to be deloused and showered. We are nobodies. Next will come the cutting off of my hair. I was allowed to grow it somewhat before I got released. If I had've stayed out, it might have reached a decent length. No decency in here. Well, fuck them. And nakedness is no degradation. We stood naked for ever before they came with their clothes. Nothing wrong with my naked bod either, man. Put a little swagger in my walk; but keep that scowl on my face. They circle around me warily. I'm getting the star treatment. Copper shooter, eh!

That nakedness doesn't last long and soon I'm in prison grey and the last of the outside disappears as my hair is trimmed back to my scalp. Now, I'm a convict. A prisoner of the state, numbered and dehumanised. Fuck it; fuck it, fuck it! To hell and back. I can't stand it. I keep collapsing into myself. Have to find something in my mind to pull me through. I'll get used to it. I will, I will!

I stand at the door of the nightclub looking real cool. My hair's slicked back just right and the curl dangles over the forehead just right. Everything's just right and I have a roll of bills in my pocket and I'm ready to groove the night away. Black pleated pegged pants; black shirt; narrow white tie to go with my long draped sports coat. Got my brothel creepers on too and I'm ready to creep. I put a little swagger in my walk as I brush past the bouncer. Him, he can't bounce. Can do him with one hand tied behind my back and he knows it, but I'm cool, you dig?

'How's it with you, Fred?' I make with the chatter as I stop a little away from him so that he can take all of me in. I pull one of the new long fags outa the pack and light up. I don't offer him one. He isn't one of us, is he?

He eyes me as if he would like to tread on me then lifts his foot cautiously and replies: 'A little quiet, but we got a new singer and she's got a voice and a bod along with it.'

'Bet you, she's not for you,' I smile as I peel off one of the bills and let it drift into his hand like a snowflake. Inside my eyes sweep over the room. I ain't one to keep in the shadows. Brown, looking good and on the prowl. I make my own space as I drift on by in my crepe-soled shoes. I sink into a chair at the front of the place. Right in front of me is the breasts of the singer moving just for me as she sings:

> 'My man wears pegged pants,
> Long draped coat and a narrow tie,
> Boy, when he gets moving,
> He makes me puff and sigh.'

Her lips move around the words and push them out at me. She starts on another verse of the song:

> 'My man, he's built so big and fine,
> Yeah, I tell you, he stands tall,
> Got, his mumma working overtime,
> Every night we have a ball.'

The waiter comes with a drink on the house. I sip and watch her fine breasts moving under the green silk of her fine dress. They're moving just for me. Man, I know it's going to be my night . . . I'm walking down that street in that posh suburb, and this kid, this girl-child with mother of course comes outa this nice neat house, all bright and clean, with a nice green closely cropped lawn around its face. Nothing outa place here excepting me. And then this kid, this girl child picks up a pebble, and lets fly with all the viciousness which lurks in the human breast. It hits me on the right shinbone. I look down at the instant scar, still hurting like mad, man. I look across at that little bitch with hate in my eyes and snarl: 'You rotten little moll, just wait till I get ahold of you.'

I hurt! I drag my leg as I move towards her, and the

white lady, the mother gets all upset and protests: 'She's just a child.' I reply, 'So am I lady and I'm going to get that little cunt'—and just then my leg collapses under me and I'm down on hands and knees, down on all fours, just a wild cat and timidly I belly level away, as that fucking little bitch picks up more pebbles and the white lady smiles and says: 'You aren't no child. You're just an animal and the RSPCA should come and put you down . . .'

I come outa my daydream and mutter, 'Well, lady, satisfied, now I've been put down?'

And the screw escorting us across to the cell block, snarls: 'Keep your trap shut.' And I shut it, for I can't daydream myself outa this one. All I do in my head is scream and scream. This is going to be my home for the next umpteen years, Christ!

2

My New Home

Now I'm an old lag, moved up into the world, become an adult and made it to the main yard. No more little juvenile. Mummy, I'm a man. I think so at least. Yeah, I am. From Cluny Boy to Freeo Man, nothing can make or break me. Do it standing on my head, if only, if only it wasn't so long. Ten years and after, help! The screaming continues and continues in my head. No way out. Never been in the army like Old Clarrie. Where to get the strength? Cluny, the shooting of that copper. The screws have been treating me a little different from last time. With respect! I ain't no small-time crim. I shot a cop. I'm violent and vicious, and someone to be reckoned with. Yeah, I am. So I slouch along beside the proudly marching Clarrie. He's back under the command of his old serge major and seems to be enjoying it; but he's only got six months. Anyone can do that standing on their head. Oh God!

A jangling of keys as the screw orders us to halt. He unlocks the big wooden door leading into the main division where I'll most likely be. Surprise! He hands us over to a screw, who hands Clarrie over to another screw, while he marches me along the division. Same old place, flagstones and three tiers of cells and the stupid wire netting stretching across the bottom from lowermost landing, right to left, to bounce off hurting objects from above. And you know what, you know what? My first time in here, the place looks huge, cavernous, now just small and dowdy, like, like a little old lady, like that old Queen Victoria who reigned when the place was built. I don't wanta spend all my time in this old-fashioned dump. It smells of the suffering men inflict on men. It smells like, like an Institution. Yeah, an institution, a House of Correction. Home, man!

March along this length of hovel and reach an end door. Halt. Again the jangling of keys. Wooden door opens. Across a little space I am confronted by a metal grille. I know what it unlocks on—the New Block. So that's where I'm going to live for who knows how long. Make it an eternity, you dig?

The New Block was built during the Second World War for soldiers and backs onto the women's section. Never been in there, the New Block, you ninny, and why am I going in there now? Questions? No answers in boob. Just commands. You get marched this way, you get put there. You get work, a tobacco ration and even a few bob a day which you can spend on what they call luxury items, such as a tin of condensed milk. They also call them privileges and they can be taken away from you, if you so much as ask a question from a screw. Well, I learnt all that before. No big deal, huh?

I wait while he opens the door; march through when he tells me to; wait until he opens the grille; march through when he orders me to. Wait until another screw takes over. Wait as the first screw locks the grille behind me. The second screw takes me to his office. Wait outside while he fumbles and lip-reads through the paperwork . . .

The New Block is a cube, you know, square like the heads of soldiers and thus unlike the dreariness and weariness I have just been marched along. Army and time has evolved beyond the old Victoriana. Only two tiers and no wire netting stretched across the bottom landing. The colour scheme is not whitewash lime but creamy nice. Somehow, it makes the place seem airy. The scream inside becomes bearable. The walls don't press so much. The doors aren't that black corrugated iron-sheeted narrowness, but in keeping with the colour scheme are creamy and of flat-sheeted metal. Lots of metal in this concrete block. Metal beams and metal struts and even a whole metal wall . . .

The screw looks up and sees me eyeing the place, and growls somehow friendly-like: 'Home, sweet home. You're in max so make the most of it.'

'Yeah,' I venture, 'just show me the way out.'

'Got a lip on you, have you?' he threatens. 'We run a nice quiet block here. Just don't step outa line. Had one bloke here, you're more or less taking his place, thought he wanted to go home. He did. Went to the main division to see the doctor, and then into the main yard. Clambered up and ran for the wall. Well, we warders are a kindly lot, got orders to fire, but to keep the first shot low, don't want to lose one of you cons. So he got his balls shot off. Kept on running somehow, and what could the poor guard do, but shoot a little higher. That was when he lost his head and we got a vacancy. So thank him. You could do a lot worse, you know.'

He goes quiet, leaving me quizzical. I glance at him looking down at his paperwork. Well, I don't wanta lose my balls, so I ain't trying for any wall just yet. Must be other ways out . . .

I like planning a job right down to the essential and even unessential details. That's how to do it. So ignore the walls. Better ways outa here, and I've had all the time in the world to find them. Reception, that's the weak spot in the defences. The police van comes and don't stop long. The crims are delivered and it takes off and out. The reception block also contains the laundry and the showers. So I wait my chance. Once a week we go there for showers and get lost in the steam and if the screw likes the male bods, his eyes latch onto the one with the longest or fattest dick, thus leaving it wide-open for me to make my move. Make sure I get a shower close to him. The water pisses down, the steam rises and the screw's eyes are fastened on that long dick. Time hisses along with the water. Soon he'll turn the showers off. No sound of the police van pulling in. So what, I've got 'the key', if not this week, the next, or the next, or, or, or . . . oh God! The motor! Sneak up on that screw. Put him to bye-byes with a king hit. Down like a log. Quickly, so quick that I catch his erection going down, I strip off his uniform coat, pants and boots. Pull them on. They fit enough. Unlock the door with his keys. Duck out. Lock the door behind me. This is my treat. Don't want any other con along for the ride. The van is there. Very much the screw, I walk over to it. The back door is open. You might call it an open invitation, but I don't accept. I duck under as it's a big old Black Maria and wedge myself between axle and body. Tight fit, but this wild cat is slim. Back door slams; the motor starts: the van rolls to and through the gates. Out! Moving down the street, turning towards Perth. Wait until an intersection. Unwedge my bod. Let it down onto the road. Up and on my feet. Wildcat's made it. Bloke in the car behind eyeballs me. I brush off my uniform, give him a wave and Wildcat is off and running free . . . but he ain't.

The big screw in the office languidly gets to his feet and reaches for his keys. 'Guess you'll be on light duties till that arm of yours heals,' he growls. 'Put you on cleaning till then.' He lumbers out and marches off as if he's on a parade ground. He expects me to follow and I do. He goes to a cell across the way, opens the door and shows what is a large room compared to the cells in the older part. There is one catch. Someone's sharing the peter. 'This ain't the Ritz,' he growls, interpreting my look. 'Space is at a premium now, and so you're to share this cell with our librarian. One of your mob, a murderer, so you'll be nice and cosy in here. Maybe you'll take each other out and save the state your upkeep.'

I gawk at him. He gets annoyed, shoves me in, then locks the door with that old familiar sound of jangling keys and the clunk, clunk as the door is double locked. I stand there just feeling the scream building up inside again. Then the peephole in the door swings open and the screw eye appears

21

to glare, to gloat, as he informs me: 'This is where that bloke who decided to check out permanently lived. He crossed your cell-mate, created a ruckus, so take this as a friendly warning of what happens to little pricks who think it grows longer when they shoot a cop. Don't get on the wrong side of Singh. Him and the Chief Warder were in the Indian Army together. The Chief a major, him a subedhar, or something like that. He loved that Indian Army and his men. Same thing here . . .' and then his eye and voice are gone leaving me on my lonesome.

Stand there. The screaming in my mind goes on and on. At last, it lowers to a level I can stand. I go to stretch my arms out full length and my mouth shrieks in pain. Forgot about that bloody broken arm. Nursing it, I turn and survey my home. Big cell. Big enough to hold two bunks with space between for a small table, single, with a bolted stool in front of it on which of all things is a neat little cushion. Think about plonking my bod on it, but hesitate. Someone else's territory? I remember what the screw said. Better be cautious. Examine the window instead. High and narrow, difficult to get up to peer out. In my last cell, I unscrewed the table, and so could lug it to the window, stand on it and stare out to the sea.

There in the distance over the roof tops, it lies glimmering in the moonlight, like the back of some fabulous huge serpent. It helps me to do my time. I fall in love with it, and when I get out, I make a beeline for the beach to say hello to that old serpent. Well, something like that, and there is this girl there. We get to talking and I get to look over her curves. She's something out of Carter Brown. Al Wheeler eyes her, running his insolent eyes along her long slim legs, the flat stomach, the overabundant curves of her breasts. He puts a smirk on his face, and sooner or later he gets what he wants. But Wheeler is a Lieutenant of Police, and what am I, but some little brown-skin ex-con not even knowing how to be on the make . . . Oh hell, can't even see the sea from this cell. I end up watching my reflection in the polished floor. I turn my attention to the two lockers at the foot of the bunks and I notice a strange thing. One of them has a padlock on it. One of those things with a combination lock so that you can't pick it easily. Well, that's the theory; but usually they're so badly made that you can snap them open with a jerk. I try, but this lock seems better made than others. I twirl the numbers trying for the right combination. No go. Then it hits me. A lock on a con's locker. Who is this con? What did the screw say: a friend of the Chief Warder and ex-Indian Army? Christ, I don't know. Best to let things roll. I eye the bunks. My God, one has sheets beneath the blankets. We don't get sheets in boob. Is this, what did that screw say, the Ritz? Suppose that's some kind of hotel. This little Nyoongah is only nineteen years old and never been out of West Aussie, so how could he know after fucking up his chances of making it to the east. The only Ritz he knows is a cafe on Wellington Street and there's nothing posh about that greasy spoon. Well, I'll just have to wait until the bloke comes. The other bunk with the folded blanket must be mine. I stretch out on it and pass the time trying to think of some girl I like. Denise was always a gas. Man, she had something going for me too.

3

Robbi Singh

I'm lying on the bunk thinking that fond memories only make you feel awful and lonely hearted, when the blokes start coming back from work. Footsteps and movements of bodies and then the jangling of keys begin as the cons are let into their cells and locked up for the night. I dunno what to do, so put myself into a sitting position and wait.

The door is flung open and by gosh and by gum my eyes near start out of my face as this, this great fat man sorta waddles into the cell. The screw waits until his bulk is in, puts his head in to check me out, then pulls the door closed quietly. Can't take my eyes off the bloke, though should. Eye contact means fights; but, well, who the hell cares, I can take a fatso any day of my term. I stare on at the bloke as he lowers his bulk down on his bunk. How does that song by Fats Domino, 'The Fat Man' go? Not one of my favourites. The bunk groans under his weight, and I swear, sags under my very eyes, not the wire netting, but the frame itself. His breath comes in little pants.

I sit and my eyes flicker up the bulk to his soccer ball head. It's the same colour as a football and his eyes are black and large and what I might call, if they belonged to a chick, sorrowful. On him they look as if they might belong to a big overweight city dog. Here Rover, here Rover. Come on, I can take you anytime. This cat hates dogs, specially great fat suburban ones. Still, he looks a bit like a Nyoongah, 'cepting I ain't seen a Nyoongah that fat before. Most of us are tall and skinny, or short and skinny. Suppose it's the grog which leaches the flesh off our bones.

'I'm Robbi Singh,' he breaks into my thoughts with a deep voice coming from deep within that mound of flesh.

'Yeah,' I say gruffly and toughly, trying to stare him down and get the edge on him, 'people call me Wildcat.'

'Yes, you wounded the police constable,' he replies in a precise English which sounds foreign, but not too foreign.

'And you're some sort of murderer,' I snarl back, sneering a little because he don't look like a murderer. He looks harmless and it might be my lucky day. I'm going to be boss of this cell. What can he do except quiver like a great lump of jelly?

'Yes,' he says slowly. 'The Chief Warder informed me that you were coming in. A bit of a troublemaker, but I expect that with some training you'll make a good servant.'

'Ain't no servant, fatso,' I grate out, 'and I don't listen to no wog anyways.'

For a big man, he sure moves fast. Before I finish speaking, he has me by the left arm and I'm dangling two foot off the floor. His fingers grip like steel and he tightens and loosens them to make his point.

'You want to have this arm broken to go along with the other one?' And he flings me back casually onto the bunk. Christ, I'm scared again. This bloke is as mean and as nasty as they come. Worse, he ain't even breathing heavily, just that short breath popping in and out of his lungs, like he was a motorbike engine on idle. He sits there gazing across at me and I feel my eyes slide away.

'The floor must be kept clean and polished; the bunks made, and the shit bucket emptied and washed out. I abhor stenches,' he says, though I can smell the musky smell of his lard, and it crinkles my nose. Now should I say 'Yes, sir' to him, or not? I nod and he continues: 'Once, you learn your duties, we'll get along. My previous cell-mate decided he wanted to escape. I got the Chief Warder to send some flowers to his funeral. Only wreath on it, I'm told. Now, I'm not a heavy master. I just expect to be obeyed.

Your arm's still in plaster, so you'll be on light duties until it mends. Still, you can keep the cell clean. Now, it's time for tea.' He goes to the locker I'd thought was mine and it's where he keeps his grub. He pulls out a half loaf of bread and a jar of jam, then twiddles with the number on the padlock of the other locker, from which he takes out a knife. This I ain't ever seen in boob before. He looks at me, then cuts a couple of slices of bread and jams them. He locks away the knife, then passes me one of the pieces. 'Part of your wages,' he says, 'but remember, I operate on a process of reciprocity: you scratch my back and I'll scratch yours, or better still, nothing for nothing, or perhaps a broken head.'

I realise that I'm dead hungry, and just then the screw unlocks the door and a con comes in to fill our mugs with steaming hot tea. Great and we munch awhile, not even listening to the sounds dwindling outside. I guess the screw is in his office, and'll be there until it's lights out at eight.

Fat Robbi finishes off his tea and bread, then groans in his deep voice: 'It's glandular, not from overeating. The doctor is no damn good and I'm trying to get to a specialist. I'm slated down for one, next week. An excellent one, I'm told, and I hope so, for the last one I consulted was no damn good. Just have to give it a go, won't I? You have to keep the dirty mugs until the morning, then wash them out carefully. I have replaced the bucket of water with a water filter container, for the splashes would mess up the polish on the floor. This room is not designed for conveniences. The British, you know, were never ones for cleanliness, not like we Indians, and so we must make do and fit in with their slovenly habits, but it is good for discipline: to make do with things as they are is a sign of virtue.'

And a sign of bullshit, I think, as I glance at him, then away. He's looking at me as if he expects an answer and after his lifting me off the ground with just one hand I hasten to supply one: 'So, you're an Indian?' I ask, dredging through my mind for the appropriate info, which I get from the encylopedia. Not much to go on. 'Like Gandhi and such like.'

'Yes,' he says settling back,'but also unlike him, for I'm Indian Army demobilised.'

'Well, what are you doing here then?' I demand.

He doesn't answer, but goes to his locker, twiddles with the numbers and opens it. He pulls out what I recognise as a crystal set with a headphone dangling from it, which reminds me that I have to apply for a headset to plug into the prison program. He looks at me and states: 'I listen to the news at this time each evening. We shall continue our discussion after it.'

And so I have to sit there trying not to look at him as he sags supine on his bunk, a beached whale. Well, his absence in the mental sense, does give me time to think. I never realised in my wildest dreams, that boob could be like this. It's not like this or wasn't like this in the juvenile section. Naw, or as far as I know, in the main division. This is something else. Strange, and maybe I can make something of it. After all, this fat old bloke, this Indian is much more than he appears. Look at what he did to me, and he's a murderer too. Must be one of the biggies in this joint. I'm lucky to be in this cell with him. Just think of the lurks I can learn. Wildcat is gonna have the know-how to be a real big man when he gets out. This university is better than that book-learning joint I stumbled on and hated when I was out. Well, I'll learn all right and then I'll get even with this fat sausage for lifting me up like that. I'll show him he can't mess with this cat. Cat can do a lazy fat old dog anyday. So I lie back just thinking about it, just dreaming about it, feeling how it'll be when I'm the big bloke, boss of his life and the lives of others . . .

Older and tougher, just don't mess with me and I might not mess with you. One time find myself without any loot. Need a few bucks to see me through. Go to a few clubs and meet a few ladies, and that takes the folding stuff, man. So a simple little job is called for. There's that pawnshop just waiting to be knocked over. And the creep who runs it is not only a fence, but a dobber-in. Needs to be taught a lesson, a hard one. I pull my revolver out from the ice box where I keep it. 'On ice,' it's a joke, get it! Well, it soon warms in my hand. I take out the six bullets and look at them. Copper-headed. Ready to explode. Pow, pow, pow! Then I put them back and check out my threads. It'll be the striped suit I picked up in the op-shop for such an occasion. Otherwise wouldn't be seen dead in it, but when you have to, you have to. And so I put it on, then think about my brown skin and how that could be a give-away. So I get gloves and then find a balaclava. Stuff them in the little bag I'm taking along for the loot and am on my way.

It's getting on to five in the afternoon, and who cares a damn for me, or what I'm about to do. This part of the city is inner not outer, and it's where the action is; but the pawnshop is real close to where I doss. There's some who say that you should never shit in your backyard, but I'm one of them who believes you should, because who in their right senses would, and this pawnbroker is so bent, he'll be too frightened to pick anyone out from a line-up. Drift along the street and take up a position across from the store. No one wheedling and begging inside. Cross quickly to the entrance of a lane next to the door. Pull on the gloves. Look out to check the scene for possible heroes and coppers. See no one. Drag the balaclava over my head and duck around and in.

The fat pawnbroker heaves up the great melon of his head. His eyes almost start out of his head as he glims my revolver. I toss the bag at him. 'Fill it up—with notes,' I grate, waving my revolver and thumbing back the hammer. He does so too slowly for my liking. He goes to pass it to me. He thinks I'm dumb. There's the safe. I'm not some two-bit punk. Quick as a flash I lock the street door, go round the counter and bring the barrel of the gun down across his face. The sight rips his face. My tongue flicks my bottom lip as if I'm tasting his dripping blood. 'All of it,' I snarl, and give him another one for good measure . . .

'If you think you can take me, try it,' a voice rumbles away my fantasy. The Indian has put away his crystal set and is standing over me. His hand rises and I flinch. He gives a laugh and collapses on his bunk. I sit up and watch his fat thighs stretching the cloth of his pants. I note that the cloth and tailoring is better than the rubbish I've got on. He's a biggie all right.

'What sorta murder did you commit?' I ask him softly.

'All murders are absurd,' he answers. 'No one can really kill a person. The soul endures and only the body is killed. But some bodies need killing and his was one of them. It is a somewhat complicated tale and begins some time ago, but since my cell-mate is no longer with me,' (and he leers slightly at this), 'such an unfortunate accident, I suppose I should inform you, seeing that I may train you to eventually take a small part in my little enterprise dealing with prison welfare.'

What the hell is he talking about? A bit loose in the scone, if you ask me. But no one is asking me, so I nod and settle back. At least, he's stopped that screaming in my head and got me thinking less about those ten years and the key. Hell, what is outside anyway, 'cepting another big prison. This one'll do for now, so entertain me like Fats Domino, my man . . .

'Well,' old Fatso settles back in an attitude that shows me that he loves talking and'll talk until the cows come home. Let him, we've both got plenty of time. 'You see,' he goes on, 'I enlisted in the Indian Army, a Punjabi regiment under Colonel Hastings, became a subedhar, and Captain Riley, he who is now the Chief Warder of this place of incarceration, was the captain of my company. During the Second World War we were posted to Malaya and when the Japanese came down like, well like the wolf on the fold, we were left behind and isolated, that is our company, for the regiment withdrew south to be bottled up in Singapore. To cut a long story short, we soon were dispersed. The Japanese were everywhere and I thought that our boys, and myself of course, might have a better chance out of uniform. Malaya has a large Indian population and we would just disappear into it; but then we had Captain Riley, who was of course a Britisher and stood out like a sore thumb. What could be done with him? Worse, he was all for fighting on, or at least keeping out of the clutches of the Japanese. Our radio still worked and I kept with the captain and we passed on messages of troop movements until Singapore was captured.

'There's one other thing, which we took advantage of, wartime conditions mean loot, or denying the enemy the means to wage war. We raided the Penang bank and saved a fair few gold bars. These I placed in the safekeeping of an Indian in Jahore. The glimmer of so much gold turned Captain Riley away from his duty. Those last radio calls to Singapore were only feints, to show what good patriotic chaps we were. After that the wireless set met with an unfortunate accident and we were on our own. My main problem remained the captain. He had to keep under cover and when he moved it had to be at night. I managed, then we, that is we Indian chappies, heard that the Japanese were recruiting an Indian corps out of prisoners of war to fight against the British for our independence. An advantage to be utilised, though not as a volunteer, but as a liaison officer between the Malay Indians, the corps and the Japanese. You see, I had concluded that the Japanese were fighting against the British, that their argument was with them and not with us.

'Eventually, I wormed into the good books of a certain Colonel Yamamoto, who saw the war as an opportunity to repair his family fortunes. He was quite a chappy and not one of your gung-ho types at all. We got a thriving black market going, and Captain Riley, forced to remain hidden, occupied his time in seeking to mend the wireless set. This, this set-up continued for a year or so, and then the Japanese began to run out of steam. The writing was on the wall, though by this time, they were dealing with anti-colonial elements all through South-East Asia. Colonel Yamamoto, for a consideration of course, decided to take across to Indonesia a consignment of arms to the nationalists there. I took this opportunity to smuggle my gold out of Malaya and also Captain Riley. We had a barge of a boat which managed to avoid any allied aircraft and as soon as the arms were delivered (along with the Colonel who had plans to go north) we sailed off and south, and hit Australia around about Broome. There we met a station owner. The Captain assumed the role of a hero and I became his faithful Indian sergeant. Unfortunately the chap found out what our box contained. We made a deal with him that if he stored the gold bars for us, as soon as we had reported in, we would return to divvy up the loot. He was all for it, too much for it; but you have to remember that I was a poor Indian and had the highest opinion of white men. They usually kept their word when they had an opportunity to share in the proceeds. I believed him. We were flown south to Perth and lauded in all the newspapers. Captain Riley was wined and dined; while I, forgotten, waited for my army pay to arrive from Delhi. It never did. While I was waiting for it, the war came to an end, and with that, our careers in the army. We were demobbed and allowed to stay on in Australia, I broke and in dire need. It was then that Captain Riley decided to join the penal service. He felt lost without a uniform, and as he was a former British officer and a hero, he didn't enter in at the ranks, but became Chief Warder.

'He used his first pay to send me north to Broome to arrange for our gold bars to be sent south. Unfortunately, the chappie in whose safekeeping they were, refused to acknowledge their existence. In fact, he called me a black bastard and ordered me off his property at the point of a gun. There was a scuffle, and alas he lay dead.

'I quickly realised that they didn't like "black bastards" up there, especially black bastards who killed white men. I couldn't say anything about the gold and so I was sentenced to life and found myself down here under my old Captain. Well, things could have been worse, far worse, and now I have settled in and we are on the way to amassing enough funds for him to return to Blighty and I perhaps to India. I might have escaped long since; but unfortunately, my old Captain with the loss of the gold lost his trust in me. In short, he doesn't believe my story. But let it be said that we as comrades in arms have carried on our relationship for our mutual benefit, though he refuses to aid in my escape. He knows I would go and search for the gold, and perhaps have better luck than he would. It must still be hidden up there.'

'Should've given your gold to the Nyoongahs,' I say, 'they would've kept it for you.'

'I suppose so, but they didn't meet us when our boat came to shore.'

I smile at him, wondering whether to believe him, or not. I might be just a kid, but I already know that cons are the biggest bullshit artists out, and if they haven't pulled off a big job, have one lined up to be done the moment they get out. Just another big mouth, I am about to decide when there is the sound of a key in the lock. Clunk clunk, the door swings open and a screw pokes his head in, withdraws it and then in comes the Chief Warder, a short stout bloke with a face that has seen a lot of whisky go down its suck hole. He smiles at the big Indian and sits down on the stool. The screw enters with a thermos flask and a cup and saucer. He pours the Chief Warder a cup of coffee and then fills Robbi Singh's mug.

'All A-okay?' the Chief asks Singh.

'He'll do,' is the reply with a nod at me. 'He'll be a cleaner until his arm's better, then I think the print shop is the place for him. Need a go-between there.'

The Chief Warder examines me as if I'm a dead rat, or something not yet rotten and stinking, then says to the screw: 'If this one gives you any trouble, put him on a charge. Supposed to be a troublemaker and we don't want troublemakers in this division.'

'I'll do just that, but I won't shoot off his balls,' the screw replies challenging his boss.

'An accident,' the Chief informs him stiffly. 'The man tried to desert and paid the penalty. He knew what he was doing,' and he stares coldly at his underling until the man lowers his eyes.

'Yes, sir,' the screw snaps, almost saluting.

I can see he is another old soldier. The whole bloody jail must be filled with them and I wonder what they do on Anzac Day. Perhaps they even have a monument scrawled with all the names of those who have fallen into this place. I begin squirming and have to command myself to sit still. It's too crazy for me. I've never even imagined that one day, or rather night, I'd be sitting in a cell while screws jawed with a prisoner. It's a little frightening, as if the world is not divided into black and white, into them and us, but shades of grey. Well, that'll suit me. Ain't got nothing to lose and umpteen years to get something to gain. Kids like me have to learn quick smart, or go under. Maybe, at last, my lousy luck is changing. I'm sharing a cell with a con who has an in with the screws. Man, I have to hang on here and learn the ropes.

4

The Welfare Lurk

The grey mouse, Robbi calls him. A prey for the wild cat. I glance at him, then away, because if you stare at him too long, he becomes all fidgety. He really is scared being amongst us murderers, would-be murderers, thieves and a lot of ex-soldiers who don't really like civilians that much.

You know, the New Block, the division is filled with them. Soldiers I mean, ex-soldiers who after the big war just don't fit in anywhere except here. They're all like me. All lost and forsaken; all dreaming of a war in which they would come out winners with enough loot, or what have you, to last out their days. And a lot of them are screamers, and a lot of them are not right in the head; but they have all been institutionalised, just like me. I came up from Cluny Boys' Home along the river to Freeo, which is starting to become a freedom of a sort. Yeah, freedom, as Robbi tells me, is found in this place, in the interstices, big word that, but I've started on my encylopedia again, and also a dictionary. 'Interstice: a narrow or small space between things or parts; crevasse.' And what I mean by that is the spaces between the discipline, between the eye-fucking, between the buttons of the screws. Easy to exist in those interstices. Who cares if you are marched here and a marched there, obeying orders with a blank face like a good soldier waiting for that chance and evading rules and regulations for your own good, and obeying them for your own good? He's a good one old Robbi, Fat old Robbi who tells me that if I'm to survive this place, I've gotta adjust, learn to function, 'Yes, sir' and not 'No, sir'. No use playing up to make yourself a big man, for these troopers have seen it all and they don't take kindly to those who try to rise above the ranks, who dirty the regiment which the New Block has become. They got a sense of pride and they mean to keep that pride, for even the screws are ex-army and like to run a tight outfit . . .

Most of this I get from Fat Robbi who loves talking and who is really a good old bloke as I've said before. He's the one who has got me sitting in front of this civilian, this Mr Reading, the welfare bloke who sits among this flock of murderers and thieves and shudders deliciously as he feels the apprehension creeping over his bones, as he relaxes feeling his tension start to ease. His grey eyes steady, as he waits for someone to begin the session. Robbi has his bulk overflowing a chair.

'What we are concerned about, sir,' he begins in that rumble of a voice of his, 'is prison welfare. I believe that when you incarcerate a man, you should supply him with the necessary means of reformation. Discipline and coercion are fine, but this end must always be kept in sight.'

'Yes, yes,' the grey mouse agrees, his grey eyes flickering from one form to another, for he dares not look us in the eyes. A slight tic begins at his right cheek, and he crosses and recrosses his legs, before suddenly pulling out a packet of cigarettes and saying, 'Smoke?' The packet moves down the table. Each convict takes one, or more, and the packet moves back to him nearly empty. He looks down in satisfaction, for this group is the best he has. He does the same in other divisions and the packet is always empty when it comes back.

A box of matches passes down and we sit back smoking. He relaxes some more, and says: 'Well, uh, my job has been somewhat ill-defined for me. I have a charter to prepare you men to eventually take a productive place in society. We talk things out, our problems and inclinations. Your worries are my concern and if you are upset about things, about your families and loved ones outside, their hardships and stresses imposed, I must stress, by the absence of the breadwinner, I contact them. My job is to ease want, to instil, I think I can say, caring into this system . . .'

He might have gone on for some time like this, but Robbi rumbles in with: 'And to reform the prison system so that we must be reformed by the system.'

'Yes, yes,' the grey mouse agrees.

'Facilities,' someone drops the word.

'A gymnasium,' another adds.

'Yes, yes,' the grey mouse agrees.

Robbi has told me that this is how the session will go. The mouse has no ideas of his own and will agree and listen and cooperate. 'That is the operative word,' Robbi tells me, ' "cooperate",' for he has as much chance in reforming us as he has in becoming the superintendent of this jail.

So I smoke my cigarette and switch off as the other blokes bring up little problems and pretend to attentively listen to his answers and tentative offers to do something. At last, it is my turn, or at least I feel that I should put in my penny's worth. So when the conversation lapses, I say: 'Sir, since coming in here, I've been thinking over things. You see, there's lots of kids like me out there. Part-Aboriginal kids,' I enlighten him, though he must have read my file, 'and not only us'uns, but other kids too who are embarked on a life of crime. Well, I've been thinking that maybe I should write a book for them. Warning them what'll happen if they keep on the way they're going.'

'Yes, yes,' he says leaning forward, his eyes on the plaster on my broken arm. It is something he can do without doing much. He leans back and away.

'I, it would mean that I could work through some of my life, find out where I went wrong,' I end rather lamely.

'It is an excellent idea,' the grey mouse replies. 'Have you spoken to the schoolteacher about it? I'm sure there are courses you could do, and naturally, I'm only too pleased to be of assistance . . .'

I nod to this, and put out my cigarette. I know the

schoolteacher. Whereas this one is a grey mouse, the teacher is a brown rabbit. He has a burrow in which we can get away from the discipline and pretend, or aspire to learn something. He bustles and hops from con to con with his rabbit's nose atwitching and his mind working out the reports on the numbers who attend his classroom. He's all for the idea, and I know, for Robbi has told me, that it'll look good on my file. 'The system is ours to abuse, or use,' he tells me, then blathers on about how a good soldier, there it is again, knows when to rush forward and when to hang back, when to thrust and when to parry. He must know the system like the back of his hand, learn the drill and let the officers know that he is a smart soldier; and this then leaves him to do what he wants to do in his own time. Well, that is how Robbi carries on. Problem is that in here we don't have that much time that is ours . . . Now, I look at him. He nods and I know it is almost time for the session to end. While I wait, I give the room the once-over.

In the war years, so I've been told, this was the guard room, or something like that. It is big enough to hold the table and chairs for twenty of us, and is at one corner of the block. On the bottom, hard against the outside wall. There is a heavy mental, naw, metal door in the back wall which is barred with a metal strip across it from which dangles a huge Chubb lock. I stare at the door. Beyond it is the outside. If I could pick both the door lock and the padlock, I'd be out and away.

My hopes make me one of the last to leave barring the grey mouse and Robbi who are deep in a whispered conversation, their heads together; the little mouse head and the large brown head which reminds me of a lion. A lion to my cat, huh!

'Well, I don't know,' the mouse murmurs. 'I know that prison reform is a necessity and that to achieve reform we must galvanise public support, but it is not strictly according to the rules. Still, well, perhaps if the replies could come through me . . . Oh, I see, they go to the Chief Warder.

Yes, if I have doubts, I could go to him, and this is the lot you want posted. Well, I'll do it again for you. Here's a carton of cigarettes. You know, with men like you, my job is beginning to mean something, to show distinct possibilities of, of bettering conditions . . .'

The cigarettes disappear under the voluminous jacket of Robbi. The grey mouse shakes his hand, then watches as he waddles out. He turns and sees me standing there. 'Begin that book of yours,' he declares rather than orders. Very much the con artist, I thank him for his support and go out into the division.

The other cons have been marched off back to their jobs. With my broken arm, I'm a cleaner which means I can keep an eye on the division. Robbi as the jail librarian has, theoretically, the run of the prison. Convicts when they finished them put their books outside their doors and he comes along, picks them up, and puts others in their place. Some leave a note wanting certain books, usually the ones with a bit of sex in them. Sometimes they get them, other times they don't. Robbi needs an assistant because he can't really climb the stairs to the landings any more. He has one. A young Korea vet who loves guns and violence . . .

As I come out of the room, I find Robbi waiting for me. I ask him about the door. He tells me that during the war that was where the guard came in. 'Could pick those locks and scoot,' I reply.

'It's also a way in,' he says, then dashes my dreams by adding, 'but there is another bar across the door outside, so even if you got the one inside off, it would still remain locked. Still, it has possibilities and I'm working on it,' he says, with that smile which says that he'll succeed.

'You mean,' I gasp, 'that you're planning to bust out?'

'No,' he says, dashing my hopes, then raising them again. 'Not just yet. This place is, is a refuge for me. What could a fat old soldier like me do out there?' And he waddles off to his library while I go and find my mop. Old Robbi and this place are a puzzle all right.

5

Falling Again

There's naked white male statues on pedestals. Greek statues as shown in the encyclopedia. The ground is paved and divided into squares and at each of the intersections of the lines is one of these statues. It is like an ordered forest, a plantation through which I scuttle. No, not scuttle, keep my belly low and sorta writhe around the pedestals and sneak-dash from one to the other. I don't know where I'm going. There's all these statues and I sneak from pedestal to pedestal, cross line after line. Nowhere to go. Gotta keep on moving.

'Hey, Wildcat,' someone calls. And I look up and see perched on the head of the statue just in front of me, Crow!

'Watcha doing here?' I ask him.

'What're you doing down there?' he smirks with his black beak and flops down onto the shoulder of the statue, then to his hand. He is thinner and less sleek than in other dreams. His feathers are bedraggled too.

'Well?' he smirks.

'Well?' I echo back at him.

'This is no place for a wild cat,' he says. 'Not much tucker around here.'

'Naw,' I answer back. 'It's the pits. Nothing here but all these old statues.'

'They make a nice pattern from above,' he hints. 'All orderly and beautiful!'

Crow spreads his tattered wings. He sure has seen better days and zooms up and up. I have to put my head right back until my neck cricks to keep him in view. He's just a dot in the sky. He sure can fly, then he folds his wings and falls and falls, spreads his wings and swoops back onto his perch. I gasp. If you can fly, you can control your falling. It becomes a part of your flight pattern.

'Gee, I wish I could do that,' I mutter.

'You can.'

'How?'

'You know how. Wait till the moon is full, and let it draw you up.'

He gives a smirk, caws and flutters up and then glides way way away. My envious eyes follow him. I want to, have to learn how to do that.

Now I'm climbing the spiral of a stairway going around and around a tower. It was made for man, so the wild cat has to spring from step to step. His legs begin aching and his breath begins panting. Still he continues going up and up. He is standing on a platform. Below him the statues surround the tower like an army on parade. The moon shines down on them and their shadows fall away in neat lines touching one another. They're all joined, all together. Perhaps he should become one of them. How does one become a statue; but he wants to fly, not be a stupid statue. He stares at the moon. He squats down on his haunches and stares at the moon. It fills his eyes. It calls to him. He goes to the edge of the platform and steps off. And he is falling, falling, falling and the scream in his head starts up again and he screams and screams. And Crow is swooping beside him, seemingly urging him to fly, or is he? A monstrous cawing comes from him. He tries to fly, but one of his wings is broken. It drags him down trailing a scream, rising, rising above the cawing of Crow . . .

There's a heavy banging on the iron door. Under my eyes it shudders and vibrates. An eye grows in its centre. It stares at me. I jerk up and look back, noticing that the light is on and that Robbi is on one elbow staring at me.

The screw outside stops his banging and laughs: 'For a moment I thought you were being murdered, haw, haw, haw.'

'Must've rolled on my broken arm in my sleep,' I lie.

'Heard worse in the war,' he growls, and the light goes off.

'The matter with you is that you lack discipline,' Robbi rumbles in a heavy whisper. 'I remember when the Japanese caught us in the open just north of Malacca. Our wounded boys were lying everywhere, but not a scream from one of them, not even a moan, and you know why, because they were trained men. Indian men trained to perfection by British officers. Warrior caste without an ounce of the woman in them. What happened to you in your sleep?'

I tell him and he grunts. 'Perhaps you should have tried to become a statue. Not a sound from them was there. All disciplined troops; but you want to join the air force. Ill-disciplined lot. And don't listen to an ill-omened crow. India is the home of methods of flying as well as of dying. It is a matter of balance, of wanting and not wanting to. First of all you have to accept where you are. No distractions in here. A perfect place to listen and learn and you're with the one who can teach you things . . .'

'How can you teach me to fly, you fat old thing?' I retort having got my courage back. 'Only a stupid dream.'

'First of all you must construct an airfield, level and flat, then you must construct an aeroplane. These are the first steps,' he says, not put out by my scorn, though I am because I remember the time he lifted me with one hand and if I rile him again, he might fulfil his threat and break my other arm, just when my right one's healing. I flex my fingers. Yup, in a day or two the plaster'll be off.

Now he gets into a sitting position. His fat old body all huddled and I'm reminded of a balloon, a hot-air balloon. It can never fly, only float, but then that would be better than falling, falling, falling. Gee, I get the willies just thinking of that dream.

'You've got to look within and find the wings of your spirit,' he says, and I stare at him in amazement. Here is this tough though fat bloke, this murderer talking about the spirit, just like one of those so-called brothers and priests in that so-called boys' home where they bashed you and beat you and even felt you up all in the name of religion and caring for your soul. Well, fuck that for a joke. Who wants to listen to this fat slob. 'No crow can teach you to fly,' he says. 'No one can stop the screaming in your head except yourself.'

'Yeah,' I say to his insights, feeling that all I want to do is lie down and get some deep sleep without a stupid dream disturbing me.

'It's simple,' he says, 'and in here, in your case, you've got all the time in the world to practise. It'll settle you down. I can't share my cell with a frightened child. It might prove dangerous for me. You know, I do things, have plans and ambitions and if you enter into a state of fright, even in a dream, the first time you're questioned you'll fall apart. I cannot accept that, so listen, or . . .'

So he's threatening me again, this great fatso. So fat that he has to stay on the ground floor. Too fat to even climb the landing stairs, and yet . . . here he is standing over me. His hand at my neck. Effortlessly, he lifts me off the ground. I try to kick him in the belly. Contemptuously, he flings me on the bed. I lie there looking up at him and at the mean look in his eyes. Can see it clear as day from the floodlight shining in through the windows. He's standing right in that square of light and the lattice work of the bars marks his face into some sort of fat gloating ghoul. Suddenly, I'm scared that he'll do me in. I'm just a kid. Can't handle some huge bloke like him. Maybe if I got his knife, I might have a chance; but he keeps that locked away. If I could get one of the table legs unscrewed, get it off and one time, when he tries to do this to me, bring it down on his head. Yeah, show him he can't toss me around like some football . . .

Perhaps he thinks that having the plaster on my right hand has incapacitated me. Don't know if he's noticed that I'm left-handed. Not that I care. I'm sure that he hasn't discovered that I've managed to get the table leg unscrewed. The table's a bit wobbly, and when he cut the bread the other night, he might have felt it, though I did try to distract him by thanking him for looking after me while my arm healed. He merely grunted something to the effect that I'd be doing it for him as soon as the plaster came off. I nodded being casual and friendly-like. Well, tonight he sits down on his bunk and begins hot airing about himself and the army and how he's got this scam which is making money and so on and so forth, and I decide to show him who's boss once and for all.

'Man, don't give me all this bullshit,' I say real quiet just like the tough guys do in the movies. 'I might be a kid, but I can see the truth through the bulldust. It's all shining there and it's just dried shit, you dig?'

He gives a start. I'm all hyped up. I know this guy fat as he is can move fast. I shift along until I'm next to the table. Suddenly, he's up and moving. Quick as a flash, I tear off the table leg and raise it over my head. Get him! His hand flashes out. He grabs that table leg and jerks it out of my hand, just as easy as can be, then makes me screw it back on. So much for fantasy . . .

'Well, I'm listening,' I say in reality time now. 'What do I have to do to learn how to fly?' He gets me to sit down on the floor bedside the bed cross-legged. I do this, and he comes to me and places his fat hands on my spine. He feels along it straightening out the vertebrae and then works on my neck and finally straightens my head.

'Sit like that for awhile,' he tells me and I do until I start to get bored and my mind begins wandering and my arm starts to hurt. 'Now,' he says. 'See if you can bring your mind to here.' And he reaches out and I feel a sudden pinprick of pain between my eyebrows. He must've pricked it with something for the pain lingers. 'Feel that and keep the mind there,' he orders me, and I do. My mind feels the pain, and the pain going, and then continues to concentrate on that spot. Easy enough to do and I sit on for awhile and my mind begins to drift away. I bring it back and it drifts away and I hear his voice saying that it is enough, but that I have to practise it every night. 'It'll calm you down,' he adds, 'and if you keep it up one night you'll find yourself flying better than any crow.'

'Yeah,' I say not convinced. 'But it has settled me somewhat, and I stretch out on my bunk and have a good night's rest. Not even one bad dream. If the nightmares go, perhaps one day I'll find myself flying, perhaps . . .

6

The Reform Movement

I learnt how to make a key out of a piece of wire when I was in last time. I do it again. It opens most doors. Now I am in the big room where we sit with the welfare bloke. Softly, like the wild cat I am, I pad to that door in the outer wall. I poke the wire in the big Chubb lock and twist it around. No go. I work it some more, and there is a satisfying click and the padlock hangs on its hasp. I take it off and lay it gently on the floor. There is still the door lock. Same as the cell locks. Piece of cake, and the bolt shifts back. Slowly, I push on the door; softly, I push on the door; heavily, I push on the door. It doesn't move. Failure. Bloody thing must be welded up. Slowly, I bring my mind to the centre of my forehead; gently, I keep it there; desperately, I seek to instil harmony, achieve some sort of peace. My breath moves slowly, my mind relaxes, and I come out of it into APT: After Plaster Time.

It's my last day as a cleaner and tomorrow I go to the printing shop. That's why I was mooning about getting through that door. Last chance, because I won't be mooching around the division any more. I'll be with the other cons putting lines on paper or some such work. At least it pays double the amount I get as a cleaner, from five shillings to ten shillings a week. Big deal—but I'll be able to buy jam and vegemite and toothpaste, which is about all we're allowed to get from the canteen. Well, in the next ten or fifteen, or what have you years, I'll be able to save up some coin—enough to get drunk, to buy a harlot and who knows what after. That's what my life outside was. Nothing to brag about; nothing to get excited about. Should get used to the inside. About the same. Maybe someone will brew some grog; maybe I'll get to like blokes; maybe I'll get used to the dump, like Robbi seems to have done. Him, me his servant? Well, he did look after me when I had this arm in plaster. Now tit for tat and all that; but am I supposed to look after him for the next umpteen years? Clean the cell? Make his bed? Cut his bread and spread his jam? Great life, huh, you dig? Maybe I'll learn the patience, the discipline enough to get a job as a maidservant when I get out after those umpteen years. Naw, I'll be so fucked up that I'll be good for nothing except coming back to this place I know and hate so well. Institutionalised, a real life jailbird. Fuck that for a joke.

Gotta learn some peace and harmony, just as Robbi says. Get my mind clear and work my way outa this dump. 'Settle your mind and you can live anywhere, especially here where all your needs and wants are taken care of. You bow out of the power equation.' So he says, but he's wheeling and dealing all of the time. Look at him there seemingly plotting what he preaches, in some Gandhi trance or other, but I know his mind is churning over some scheme or other. He's one of the biggies and he can lie still and no one will overtake him. Even asleep he's playing those power games to gain as much as he can. He can win a lot too, because he's got an in with the screws. Army to army, and the Chief Warder's his co-respondent, or something like that, so he can do almost everything, except rock the boat and bring the Super down. I respect him. He knows how to work the system in here. Even got a bodyguard. Young chap, ex-army of course, but Korea. More about him later, because while I'm sitting here, might as well think about my book.

I ask Robbi, 'Where do I start?' and he replies: 'Why not start at the end?' I think about that, then take it along to the welfare mouse and ask him. He says, 'What do you mean?' And then it comes to me. 'I want to show how it is when the young convict is released and there is nothing on the outside for him. He's lost; he misses jail; he ain't got no place to go. All he can see in his head is this place beckoning him back.' And you know what he says to me, you know what? 'The first thing which you must do is tidy up your English; the word is "isn't", not "ain't".' 'Yeah' I reply, 'but what about the storyline?' 'It may need some refining,' he half agrees, 'but I suggest you should have a talk with the schoolteacher and let him find you an appropriate course to do.'

So I go to the teach. The school is right down the other end of the prison. Through door after door and screw after screw. The old divisions look tatty and small. I'm glad to be in the New Block. Well, I get to First Division, my old stamping ground, and there are a new lot of delinks pushing mops and brooms along the landings. Ignore them. I've made it to the big league. Yeah, ten flaming years and the key is a big enough sentence for any man. The little screw I hate, is nowheres in sight. Expect he's on guard duty, or something like that. They don't seem to change the screws around that much, except they each have to stand a stint of duty on the wall. Well, must be a good view from up there. Hope the cunt falls and breaks his neck.

I tell the screw that lets me in, that I'm on the way to the school. The lazy sod just nods, then ignores me. Lucky, I'm an old lag and know the way, otherwise he might have to find some energy to escort me there. I leave him sleepily scratching his balls, hope he's got the pox, climb up the stairs to the first landing and go into the schoolroom where a number of cons are hanging out, bent over benches, or just leaning back and staring out at the far wall. The teacher as I've said is a brown rabbit whereas the welfare bloke is a grey mouse. He's got a crumpled brown suit on and brown hair and brown eyes and his skin is sorta sallow. He looks beaten down, and looks even more so when he looks up and tries to hold my gaze. I swear his nose twitches.

I studied the Junior Certificate under him, and I expect that when I got out he thought I would go straight. Well, I did, didn't I? Yeah, straight back inside, man! My imagination could never fit me into anything out there. Christ, I've never even had the time to find out what it's really like. What does a kid who's been in an orphanage, out for a year or so, then into boob, know about the straight world? How to imagine myself a captain of industry, or something like that? Why, I've never even met a captain of industry, or a politician. I've only met teachers and preachers, do-gooders and bad-doers, and when I sit down and let my mind drift, it settles on the bad-doers. So can I help it, if I'm one of them? Can't find anything else I want to be. Still, I have to keep busy and this writing lark'll fill my days for a while. Besides, you can mooch off in the schoolroom.

Teach twitches up at me and his rabbits' eyes glaze sorrowfully as I fill him in on my plans. He nods and squeaks and stutters, then goes quiet as he thinks. I tell him that the welfare bloke said that I should learn how to express myself a bit better. He agrees with that and hops to his files, leaving me standing there by myself, thinking of my old uncle and how good his rabbit stew is. I lick my lips as I eye him looking through the courses on offer. My old uncle, the rabbiter, would have skun him and had his skin stretched out in the sun to dry by now. 'English Expression,' he squeaks. I wrinkle my nose in agreement, then begin to tell him my plans for the book. He ain't interested. He twitches a form in front of me. I fill it in. He says that it'll take a few days for the course material to arrive. He'll pass the word along when it does, then I can come once a week and study in the schoolroom. I twitch my nose and leave. Robbi might be pleased, for now I can get around the divisions too and that may be useful; but as for the course—maybe instead of playing the fool, I should've looked at the list and seen if something better wasn't on offer. How will a course on English expression help me to write a book? I bitch to Robbi about this and he has an answer just as he has an answer for everything. He tells me I should read the modern classics. I ask him what are modern classics? He replies: 'Sartre and Camus'; and not to appear dumb, I say 'Oh,' before remembering from that short time out, Samuel Beckett, and I say his name to show that I know what a modern classic is. I ask him if the books are in the library and he says, 'No.' 'Well,' I snarl, though after the couple of times Robbi's flung me around, I'm a bit wary of losing my temper with him, 'how can I read these so-called modern classics?' And he tells me that if I ask nicely, he'll see what the welfare bloke can do. Seemingly contrite, I ask his advice on which author to start with. He replies, 'Camus; his *Outsider*.' And I ask: 'Why?' And he says because it is about a chap who's a bit like me. 'He kills his mother and ends up in prison where he is to be executed, and he feels nothing at all about it.' Then adds the punch line: 'And because it's in the library.'

'I'd never kill my mum,' I retort.

And he corrects himself: 'Neither did he, he killed an Arab on the day his mother died, and they blame him because he's so cold and instead of mourning, he makes love to his girlfriend on the day of his mother's funeral.'

'Well, that's life,' I exclaim.

And he answers: 'Precisely.'

Then I think over it and say: 'But the reason I'm doing this book is to show that I have reformed, that I have remorse . . .' He shrugs his great fat shoulders as if to say 'You work it out,' so I give it up as a bad job, and start going over the beginning in my mind; I want it to be cool, man. Cool and distant. Like us bodgies have style and so it has to have that, doesn't it?

So these things I'm going over, and forgotten is the fixing of my mind in the space between the eyebrows, or what have you. Got too many things to get together, to mull over, and I'm lying back on my bunk when there is that jingle-jangle of keys and with a great vibration of metal the door is pushed open to admit the night screw and the Chief Warder. They ignore me as always. Robbi lets his legs fall on the floor and their weight pulls his body into a sitting position. The Chief, as equal as you please, sits down next to him. I stare at this travesty of the screw–con relationship. I find it shocking. Can't get used to it. Never will be able to get used to it. This time the screw with the thermos sits on the stool. I lie still on my bunk hoping that they'll go away. They don't. The screw goes into the coffee pouring routine while the Chief talks to Robbi in a soft voice, just above a whisper. Very few words can I hear. I half close my eyes and peer at them through the lashes, catching a bundle of letters passing from chief screw to chief con. The night duty screw refills the cups then Robbi's mug. He passes the cup, then the mug, and settles back to his own. More muttering between the two. The screw finishes his coffee and goes to the door. Man, I can recognise a look-out when I see one, or as these blokes would probably say: a sentry.

While he is looking out, Robbi heaves his bulk onto his legs. He goes to the locker, bends down with great difficulty and twiddles with the combination. The other day he was taken to the specialist in Perth and returns with a bottle of pills, two of which I have to give to him each evening. I hope they work. He takes up too much room and his body gives off this smell of rancid fat which tickles my nose. Well, he manages the bending business and comes up with an envelope which he gives to the Chief. Man, was I dumb when I was a juvie in First Division. Everything was so simple then, just like me.

Well, the coffee break is over and the screws are doing their rounds. I listen to the jingle-jangle of their keys; the clump of their boots moving away, and the steady click-clicking of cell lights being switched off. Naturally, ours isn't. We have what is called studying privileges and the light stays on to nine o'clock. I look at Robbi and wonder if he'll enlighten me as to the letters. I'm left to wonder. He goes to the cupboard, pulls out two thick ledgers, then sits at the table with his back to me ripping open the envelopes and entering what might be names and addresses into one of the ledgers. The other is used, I swear it, to enter in a pile of, of cheques. Man, if I was standing, I would be falling. Cheques in this dump, in this house of correction!

The pile steadily grows and eventually Robbi finishes entering what I take to be the amounts in his ledger. He closes it, puts the cheques in one envelope and places them in the cupboard, then pulls out a pile of paper and envelopes. He comes to me, thrusts them in my hand and says, 'Now it's time to earn your keep. These letters are to be answered. Just copy this form letter. I stare at it and see that it has a letterhead reading THE PANOPTICON PRISON REFORM SOCIETY. The letter thanks the person for his/her donation and hopes that he/she will continue to support the worthy cause.

I stare at him and ask: 'What is this, this panopticon?'

He waves his hand around: 'This.'

'You mean the cell?'

'No, the entire prison system, including that . . .'

'You mean the peephole?'

'Precisely.'

'And all else?'

'Yes, and I even extend the system beyond the walls.'

'The outside?'

'Definitely, Australia was founded on the prison system.'

'But what has that got to do with prison reform?'

'It means to use the system to remake the system.'

'Yeah, but who gets the money?'

'That you need not know at this time,' and he stands behind me and his huge hand flops on my head weighing it down so that my eyes fall on the letters. 'Your one and only task, at present, is to copy these letters and address them.'

'I know it's some kind of scam,' I blurt out, before

beginning my task. Old Robbi is as crooked as you can be, and reform is the last thing on his mind. But to work a scam from the can. That I can admire. He's a big'un all right. The peephole in the, in the . . . I read the letterhead, 'the panopticon'.

7

Doing Time

'Time, gentlemen, time,' and after you down your drink you'll be out in the warm evening air, and the stars'll be above you, maybe the moon, and you'll be with a few mates, or with a girl, and you'll continue on to a park and sit there sipping, or kissing—whatever the opportunity is. But in here for me, there is no 'Time, gentlemen, time!' The whole of my life, ten years and the key, a sentence of indetermination, is the whole of your life when you are just going on twenty, or is it twenty-one now. I forget, for time just continues, unbroken and unwanted. Days drag; months drag; years drag, and all we know is Christmas, Easter, Sunday, the breaks in the routine. The soft flow of eternity about my forehead and it hurts, pains, and I have to keep that scream down in the centre of my forehead and let flow the segmented days of my time.

Segmentation, disciplined chunks of time. I'm thankful for it in a way. You need it to survive. Routine, sweet, sweet boredom. Your day is taken care of in hours and half-hours. Seems like there's nothing in between. At 7.00 am there's the loud sounds of the doors being flung open and you get up. I take the shit bucket down to the yard as well as my towel. Stand in line and empty the bucket, wash it out well with phenol, then try to get rid of that smell as Robbi doesn't like it in the cell. Robbi's become more difficult. Time has started to drag for him and he gives in to it, or snaps at it, like a dog with fleas. It's got him by the balls too. Then wash my face and hands. At 7.30

the gate of the yard is flung open and in we troop with
our buckets and find outside our doors a plate of cold porridge
and a mug of tea and a half-loaf of bread. Our breakfast
and bread ration. In we go and eat or discard the porridge,
and I forget about cleaning the enamel plate, difficult not
to splash with the water container and its top; but that's
what Robbi wants and what he wants, he gets. When it's
8.00 am the doors are flung open and we line up for rollcall
before marching off to our jobs. I'm in the print shop now
and it's okay. I mean I started shuffling bits of paper, then
got put on an ancient machine which lined sheets of paper,
thus acquiring a skill good for a print shop of 80 years ago.
After that, I learnt how to ink the nibs which draw the
lines on the paper sheets passing on rollers under them. That
was a skill too, for too much ink blotched the paper and
brought the supervisor down on you. After that, I became
a compositor. Another skill and it was interesting, lining
up type fonts in a row, making sure the types were of the
correct size and then stacking them into a frame to build
up a block. The block is then placed in a machine which
was, is like us. It goes back and forth, like, like the closing
jaws of a mechanical purse and you drop the paper in nice
and square and out comes the copy.

I print out a few dozen sheets of Robbi's form letter on
that machine, then stash them down my waist and bring
them back to the cell. This is before Robbi takes an elevator
down into the dumps where not even The Panopticon Prison
Reform Society exists. No discipline that's his problem. So
at 11.30, it's back to the cell block for the main meal of
the day. You line up and the screw on duty runs his eyes
over us, deciding whether to body-search each one, a few,
or none. It takes time and even the screws are slaves of
the schedule, so he merely grunts an order and escorts us
across to the main cell block where we wait at the door
while he rings the bell and then the screw inside unlocks
the door, and we pass through and the door is locked behind
us. We are marched to the big main division yard and left

to our own devices until twelve. On the dot the bell peals. We are lined up and escorted to our respective divisions, pausing at the doors to pick up our dixies which contain not much food to salivate about: meat and vegies and a cold, cold greasy soup; but what do you expect in boob? Sausages and mash? Well, we get that on Sunday, or is it Saturday? Hard to keep track of the days, the months, the years, the centuries . . . oh fuck! It's the schedule which matters.

At 1.00 pm cell doors crash open, one after another. Line up. Checked out. No one is ever missing. March through the door into the main division where we join the others to split up for our work places. Great, huh? And we loaf on and work to 3.30 pm and we're lined up and this time searched for there's a half-hour to do it in, and by the time we're at the door, and through the door, and split up and in the door and through the door and into the division, it's four o'clock. We line up outside our cells and two screws come along. Two just in case the routine has worn us down into insanity or violence. Really, it has the opposite effect: apathy and numbness. A con comes along with a bucket of tea and slops some into our mugs, and we're locked away in our cells until morning, when the whole routine will commence again. By 8.00 pm lights are out for most of the cons; 9.00 pm for us studious ones. And so it goes on and on day after day, year after year, eternity after eternity, scream after scream. No wonder some of the cons lash out to break through. If this is a hell of a routine, seven days in solitary will make it seem like freedom. Twenty-eight days and you're ready to sing and dance, if singing and dancing were allowed. Well, that might've been me last time in boob when I had this little sentence. Didn't care a stuff then because I was dumb. Didn't know about the file they keep on you, especially a bloke like me on the Governor's Pleasure. Your good deeds and your bad deeds, your attributes and attitudes are entered into that file. After the definite sentence, in this case when ten years is over, then comes the time to count up all the good points and bad points of this wild cat. Is he to be awarded the key for a while longer, or has he shown that he is ready to throw it away for good? 'It depends on you, little brother, it depends on you,' so says Robbi, and I believe him. 'You have to be a good boy,' he tells me when he was talking half the night away and was fat and sleek and filled the cell with his smell which tickled my nose.

And I follow his advice and thus the course I'm doing. No, I've done that one. Now I'm studying for the matriculation and showing that I'm well on the way to reforming. Also I've got my book under way. It begins: 'Today the gates will swing to eject me alone, alone and so-called free.' How else to start. When you're in here, the main thing you want to do is get out, and when you're out, the main thing is to get back in. Just like old Clarrie. He did his four and a half months, he got all the remission, marching and saluting, and got out, and what do you think is the first thing he does? He goes and flashes his wrinkled old cock at some sheila at the bottom of the roadway leading from the gates. The silly bird, as if that old thing could be a threat, screams her bloody lungs out, with the result that poor old Clarrie, the old digger, is back inside to continue his endless yammering about when he was in the army and one of the first to land in Anzac Cove.

'Look,' I tell him. 'You've got an army pension and all. Why don't you, when you feel like flashing, just go to a harlot and pay her? She'll let you do all the flashing and even scream, if you want her to.'

He nods his silly old head to my advice and then tells me: 'That flare went up from the funnel of that tug and it scared us shitless, cobber, scared us shitless. You know the Cove, mate, it was about the size and shape of this exercise yard. Crowded with blokes roaming about; with the wounded lying about; with the officers shouting about. Gaba Tepe was on your left. Jacko Turk had a gun there. Used to let fly at us every now and again. On your right was the Nibbruness, and we were squashed between. We came down, in a fatigue party for supplies. Usually had to wait around for a spell. That's the army for you. Wait and wait and then it's on. In the cove though, we could make use of that time, dicker for some rum if the sailors were about. They wanted souvenirs, badges, Turkish money, things like that. More than once I came back with my water bottle filled with rum. Them were the days.'

'Yeah, what else is new,' I say, thinking again of the battle of Pinjarra and my great-grandfather. I wonder if they, after the killing was done, had collected souvenirs too. A few spears, kylies, digging sticks, blood-stained kangaroo skin cloaks.

'You should see my medals,' he says. 'Whole row of them . . .'

'Well, where are they?' I demand.

'Pawnshop, cobber,' he says.

'Next time put yourself in the fucking hock shop,' I reply and drift away from him, for to tell the truth, he ain't one for laughs, or am I for that matter. I see myself as he is, as I will become after ten years and then waiting on the prison board to make up its mind whether I'm a good enough risk to be ejected out on society. 'Society, and I don't owe it a thing.' Sentence from my book which is going along in fits and starts. Who cares, I've got all the time in the world. I ain't going nowheres. Just going to become an old lag like Clarrie. You know, get so used to the discipline, to having my life ordered that I can't exist in that big prison farm outside where the sky is the division roof; the houses are the cells, and the streets the exercise yards, all lit up at night just like here, so that the screws, the coppers, can keep an eye on you.

That's what the outside is, man; but then if it is like that, why am I suffering in here? Still, I suffered out there too. What would Clarrie sing? 'Pack up your troubles in your old shit bag and smile, boys, smile the while.' Yeah, and he sings it, or better yet, 'Roll out the barrel' when he marches around and around the yard. Good for him, bad for him. Someone always threatens to thump him if he doesn't shut up.

It seems that we're all down a bit these days. The sort of hope that Robbi inspired in me, in others too, is going, gone along with his fatness which drips from his bones as I watch. Man, at last he got his desire and the fat is leaving, but taking along with it his good humour and his urge to do things. He argued with the Chief Warder and he don't come to see him any more. The letters are coming in, or going out via the grey mouse. I'm keeping that going for him. 'Involve the most people you can, in your commissions and omissions,' Robbi used to say, as he passed over the proceeds of the con, to be banked by his best mate, his old officer, the Chief Screw. Now that source of relief has dried up, has trickled away with his fat, and he just lies on his bed most times, staring at the ceiling. He's become one of those Beckett characters, the one who took to his bed and never moved. I like old Watt myself, dragging himself through the prison of the world. 'Hope, that's movement for you.' I tell Robbi, and he urges me to re-read *The Plague* by Camus. I do. Yeah, contagion all around; but the bourgeois creeps don't move me. Too fancy. Too square. Maybe it's the problem of those sorts of writers. They skip from subject to subject, just not settling down anywhere. First he wrote about this bloke, real bodgie-like, then from *The Outsider* to a lot of dreary people discussing the plague. Seems like he forgot about the cons, and the pretty boys and girls fucking themselves silly on the beaches. Man, I could dig a beach right now . . .

How bright the sun shines. It's one of those beautiful warm days for which Perth is renowned. I'm barefoot, barechested, shirt flapping in the sea breeze as I wander along the deserted beach, and I come across this chick asleep, or something. White girl, you know, dark hair, long tanned legs like a light-skinned Nyoongah, and in one of those, what do you call them, bikinis. The bottom is pulled down low so that the cleavage of her arse is showing, and the top is undone. I make a circle around her, and come back, then go up to her, flop down and make with the patter. Got nothing to lose. No response. Must be asleep. I raise my voice. The chick doesn't want to be disturbed. I sit next to her and throw some sand on her back, expecting her to react. No dice. I touch her, and she is as cold as the day is warm. I touch her head, then turn her face towards me. Christ, she's dead! Her blue eyes stare up beyond me as blank as the sky. What can I do?

So much for daydreams. Even my fantasies are nightmares in this place, though come to think of it, there's this bloke who came across this woman's corpse on the beach and, as they say, had his way with her. Yuck, with a corpse. Disgusting, I tell you. Imagine turning that body over, touching the cold clammy breasts, sliding the bikini pants down over that rigid stretch of woman flesh. Feeling the disgust as you push into that dead woman flesh and then going to town. Just a doll, a dead doll. The things you get to dream about in boob are as bad as some of the blokes you meet in jail, are as rotten as some of the things the blokes have done to land them in here . . .

I'm not like Dick, Robbi's bodyguard, the psychopath, he calls him. The one with the love of guns and violence. He's a good bloke for all that, though a bit high strung, and'll wallop you for hardly any reason at all. He began that caper on me and I slugged him back. We hammered each other, until the screw in the office shouted for us to stop the commotion. We did, or rather I backed away. I didn't want to be fucked over and get a dirty mark on my coversheet. I gotta be a good little boy, and say 'Yes, sir' to all the petty shit that goes down; but when it's safe I give that Dick a few nasty wallops and even knock him down a few times. I think he's not much of a fighter, that is until Robbi tells me that the bloke's been in the commandos and could kill me with a few fingers stuck into my sternum. 'Christ,' I say, 'and I've been doing a few rounds with the bloke.' 'Well,' Robbi says, 'he likes to knock around his comrades a bit, and likes his mates to hurt him a bit too. It's his way of loving the world.' 'Christ,' I reply and leave it at that. Trouble is that I like Dick and now I'm wary. Even when he becomes a bit difficult and we trade a few punches and I lose my temper and knock him down, I'm all the time conscious that I might be committing suicide. Well, as Robbi says, 'That's life,' and we might consider it part of Dick's sex life rather than his use and abuse of punishment. Well, at least this story is better than the beach one, and you can ease into it like you can ease into a wet cunt.

A beautiful car is like a Nyoongah girl just going on sixteen. Warm and sexy with power under her clothes. Sometimes a little stiff on the clutch; sometimes a little slow to start; sometimes outa her mind with anger and a will of her own, but something you can enjoy. I find such a car, new and dark as I am. She makes me feel good. I know I'm going places. Amen! My hair is oiled and slicked down and back just right; my black clothes are new; I've got a pair of the new winkle-pushers on my feet, and a leather jacket draped around my shoulders. I cruise down William Street all casual, but there must be a funeral for the streets are empty of dark faces. I go past the park. A cop car cruises through it and I get outa there not fast, but slow. Never panic, act like this beautiful car is yours and they'll believe it.

So nothing doing there and I wheel into the city, along St George's Terrace and am passing a bus stop when I see this white chick yawning out at me. I pull over and ask her if she'd like a lift. Her eyes weigh me up and are on the verge of dismissing me.

'Wanna drive?' I offer. 'I'll drop you home.'

She looks along the street. It's winter and that cold wind which you always get in the Terrace is shivering her skin. It decides her. She gets in, saying: 'But I gotta get home by eleven. You don't know me Mum.'

'Sure,' I reply, 'it's only nine now. That gives us two hours.'

I put on the heater to make her feel warm and cosy, and go through the city again. She looks out at the cold world, and snuggles down in the seat next to me. I turn along Wellington Street and go towards Subiaco.

'Wanta see the city lights from King's Park?' I say, and not waiting for her reply, I turn off and pass through into the park. There's a nice quiet parking spot where you can see the lights of the city gleaming across the dark serpent of the Swan River. The trees of the park rustle in the wind and the heater smoothes my way. We snuggle a little and then get into the back seat. Light a cigarette and wait while she gets her clothes off. She has some trouble or other, and then there is her huge arse shining in the moonlight. It is so fascinating to me that I take the cigarette and touch it to her bottom. She jumps like a scalded rabbit, and snaps: 'Why'd you do that?'

That's one of Dick's stories, and shows how blokes can get into your mind and affect your fantasy life. His ending would be him fucking her over her protests with her on the top because of the burn on her behind. That's what Dick is like, though most likely he would've shown her his gun by then to scare her, or impress her, or just to get her in the mood. He's into pain, that bloke . . .

Well, that little fantasy cheered me up a bit; but not all that much because Robbi is losing weight and with the weight he's losing what it takes to survive. He used to be a talkative bloke. He used to teach me things, and now he just lies there shedding his fat. Once he was so sleek and mean, so in control of it; but now he's becoming a living skeleton. His skin hangs on his bones and underneath there doesn't seem to be any muscles or tendons and those things. Just a sack of skin draped over a framework of bone.

He gets me to massage him so that, as he says, the skin will shrink and tighten over his bones. I do the massaging, and pummel and pound his body. I take a handful of skin in my hand. It lifts real easy away from his bones, and while I'm doing it I think of how my old Uncle used to skin rabbits. I remember how he used to cut the skin at the neck and legs, then with a quick jerk pull the skin off in one piece. I could do the same with Robbi's skin, or skin him like a sheep. That's different. You slash down the belly and chest; but to do it right you need a knife sharp as a razor . . .

Robbi is so depressed that it's easy to get his knife. Besides as I now do the cutting of the bread and the spreading of the butter and jam, I often have it. So one time he forgets to take it from me and lock it up. Now I have it and sharpen it on the concrete floor until the blade is all honed down and the edge can split a hair. So the next time I massage Robbi, I pull up his skin along the back bone and see how slack it comes off the bone. Run the blade down along the spine, then peel him like a banana. A slash around the neck and around the knees, turn him over and jerk it off. There lies Robbi a skeleton with a normal head and legs below the knees, but the rest of him just bare bone. Sure would look funny. I take the knife and do it. Robbi stares up at me and says: 'Now look what you've done. You'll just have to stitch it back on.'

End of daydream and I pummel his body, feeling the skin hanging from his bones: 'Maybe Robbi, those tablets of yours weren't a good idea. You're wasting away.' He grunts and doesn't answer. I say: 'Maybe you should eat more.' He grunts and that is all. I keep doing my job, feeling more and more depressed. After all, this bloke has helped me and now here he is a shadow of himself. Boob is sucking away at him, draining his vitality.

'How long have you been in?' I ask him.

He grunts, 'Ten years,' and that explains it. Been in too long and losing the will to live. Some blokes become, what do you call it, institutionalised, and get used to being locked up. Their world is enclosed by four walls. They settle in, but Robbi never has. He's had rackets going and had the Chief Screw as a pipeline to the outside. He's had his crystal set and the news to keep the prison at bay. Now, at last it's hit him. He's in the can just as we all are; and he's doing it hard! Hope he snaps out of it in time, for he's a good bloke he is. I even forgive him for thumping me on more than one occasion.

8

Yarded

Poor Robbi, still wasting away, and it seems that the whole block is wasting away with him. I'm down in the dumps and so is Dick, who is on the verge of looking around for a new master. You know, he likes playing the bodyguard, escorting Robbi wherever he goes, keeping an eye on his cell, and hanging out in the library. He likes all this. It gives him a purpose in boob. If he was just another con, just another number in the roster, I'm sure he would snap and be spending more time in solitary than out of it; but with Robbi and his schemes, he has someone to look up to, someone whom he respects to take orders from, someone to give purpose to his life. He feels that he's got an important place in a gang, or should I say, is the corporal in the platoon, and so manages to keep himself together. 'Who cares about boob?' he tells me. 'Been in one boob or another all me life: in the army, in the school, at home where that so-called dad of mine used to lash out at me for just being alive. He used to belt me up something awful, then one day he hit me, and I whacked him back and again and again. It felt good that, then lit out before he could get the coppers after me. He was a cunt through and through.'

I nod and agree with this, because I feel the same way not about the dad I never knew, but about the world around me. When I was a kid in that country town, when we walked down the street we could feel eyes on us, on me and mum and sis, weighing us up and judging us. We were Nyoongahs and so their judgment came down heavily on us. They were watching and waiting for us to do something strong, and when we did, they got rid of us without much fuss. And after that it was the orphanage and that was more than eyes on me. It was surveillance and organised same as in here. As the Bible says: 'Watch and prey lest you enter into temptation,' and so they watched and caught us in temptation. Remember one time, you know how it is with young blokes growing up and finding their penises swelling in the morning and swelling at the most inopportune times. Well, what could we do, but find some relief amongst ourselves?

So I was lying on the sand in a sandpit. But first I have to explain that Perth is built on sand and the orphanage was built on sand and right next to the Canning River, and we, meaning generations of boys used as slave labour, had constructed a sportsground beside the river. Away from it the land rose to the buildings and to keep the rise from caving in and the buildings from crumbling, us boys had constructed walls of sandstone, and below these walls, at a few places were patches of sand, sterile sandpits hollowed out on which nothing grew, but us kids liked playing there. They were a refuge from the surveillance. The hollows hid us from most prying eyes, though some of the windows looked down into them.

Well, I was lying there in the sun, just relaxing when one of my mates, a kid called Sammy, or something like that, came up and we started messing around, and soon it grew, well, a bit sexual and we were feeling each other's cocks, then jacking off. Just kids' stuff. I remember my sperm spurting out to soak into the sand and Sammy's sperm following a few seconds later. Well, now we were at ease and feeling good. We went off to kick a football around. Nothing to it; but eyes had seen us. That night, they loved doing this, those so-called brothers who had our best interests at heart, well, that night when all the kids were tucked up in bed, they came for me and Sammy. We were paraded downstairs to the common room for the full treatment.

'You were seen committing an act of gross impurity this afternoon.'

I always brazened things out because really I had nothing to lose. Six or twelve of the best, what did it matter? I shot a glance at Sammy and said: 'No, sir.' I didn't want to be insolent, and without the 'sir' you were insolent.

'Lying added to your other sin. You were observed in the sandpit below the classroom windows.'

'We were just fooling around, playing in the sand,' I say, and Sammy backs me up.

'An incorrigible rascal,' the interrogator remarks to the other members of the inquisition in attendance. He takes out his strap, caresses it like, well, like a penis, and tells me to bend over. Whack, whack, whack. 'I'll teach you not to lie.' Whack, whack, whack. 'You filthy little sinner.' Whack, whack whack, and he loses his temper and the strap is not enough for him. He throws me around the room and uses his fists and shoes. 'Teach, teach, teach you if I have to kill you,' he puffs, beating the living daylights outa me. Finally, one of the other brothers intervenes and I lay there getting my senses together. I feel the pain, but no contrition, maybe hatred, for all I want to do is flog that bastard until he pisses his pants, just as I've done. I'm filled with rage and pain and I'm silent with rage and hate.

They send me off to bed, and as I go I hear the sound of the strap going whack, whack, whack, whack, whack, whack. Six times and that's all Sammy gets, for he becomes scared and goes through all the rigmarole you have to go through, such as 'I'm sorry, I won't do it again' and 'He made me do it,' and so on and so forth. I lie in my bed waiting for him to come back and when he does, he comes sniffling to me. We hold each other and do it again. It's the only revenge we can have against those prying eyes. 'Fuck them,' I moan as I come all over the sheets . . .

Well, that's life and now I'm, what do you call it, incarcerated again, and life is a Beckett dreariness and Robbi is wasting away, and Dick is becoming mutinous. It's all falling apart. I begin hearing, just faintly, the scream in my head. Something has to give, and it better happen soon, or who knows what mess we'll get into.

So it's Saturday and that means no work. We also get to use the canteen where we can buy jam, butter, or vegemite, and cigarette papers to go with the quarter-ounce of tobacco of our ration. We line up and I ask Robbi if he wants anything, but he doesn't even nod. I get some plum jam for him and a couple of folds of cigarette papers for myself. I get my tobacco ration and join the other cons waiting to be escorted into the main exercise yard. Dick gently guides Robbi over to me. We stand on either side of him. He's a bit out of it and absently clutches his tobacco ration in a claw-like hand. A bit stupid, for it is not unknown for a con to snatch the tobacco and then dare the bloke to get it back. They won't do it to Robbi, not while Dick and me are with him, but it does dare fate a bit.

We are marched to the entrance of the main exercise yard and the screw goes through the jingle-jangling key routine. It used to bug me, but not any more. Doors upon doors all locked and windows with bars are what we're used to. We're ordered through into the yard and the screw locks the gate after us. As I've said before, most of the blokes in the New Block are ex-army and feel above the rest of the cons who are just a lot of civilians who couldn't use a gun if their lives depended on it. So they enter what they might consider enemy territory and bunch at the entrance for a while to feel out the field. Then with that ritual over, they drift off to join in card games, or hand tennis, or chess, or draughts. Another Saturday in boob, and it's the same as all the other Saturdays all lined up in rows of years . . .

Dick and I follow Robbi as he wanders over to a wall and slides down it, to sit and gaze out at nothing. We roll cigarettes and puff away. Real boring! Then this bloke comes over as if he was our best friend and beams a smile at us. For a moment, I think he's a queer, for he appears dapper, though he's in prison grey the same as us. He holds his tobacco ration in his hand and juggles it up and down. Our three pairs of eyes follow it as if it was a roll of bills. I think that he wants to exchange it for something but he says: 'Hey, you blokes you wanta get in on this game? Win yourself enough tobacco for a month of Sundays?'

Dick is about to tell him to fuck off, but Robbi comes alive and asks: 'What sort of game?'

The bloke's eyes reach out and hold Robbi's. His hand goes up and down, up and down, tossing up and catching that packet of tobacco. 'It's easy enough,' he says. 'Simple mathematics. The first blokes who get in always get their payment. I kid you not. It's as waterproof as an Omega watch.' He jerks his wrist and his eyes glance down as if he's been used to wearing an Omega all his life. He tosses the tobacco up and down. Our eyes watch it. 'You blokes in?' he asks.

'Why not,' Robbi replies, jerking his head to me. I toss the bloke the packet. 'Well, what do we haveta do?' I query, watching my tobacco ration disappearing.

He doesn't answer me, he looks at Dick who begins tossing his tobacco ration up and catching it, hard eyeing the bloke, who isn't put off by the stare. Finally, Dick flips his wrist and the packet leaves his hand. The bloke catches it, halves it, then passes it back. 'Three outa three, ain't bad,' he says, 'and no worries, eh? For those who are first shall receive their reward.'

'Well, what is this game?' I demand, looking at Robbi who's showing some interest in something at last. He seems to inflate a little, and his eyes are sharp waiting for the bloke to explain.

'Well, it's like this,' the bloke begins. 'It's a pyramid thing. I'm at the top seeing that I was the one to put my tobacco in first, then you two,' his eyes move from Robbi to me, 'are below me, and him,' he flashes a glance of dislike at Dick, 'he'll be the next to score. But what we have to do now is make up the rest of the pyramid, that means we have to get twelve other blokes, and put down when they come in, that's important because as I've said it's first in first out.'

'I see,' Robbi says in his hollow voice. He looks around and catches the eyes of New Block blokes who stop what they're doing and drift on over. He soon has twelve blokes there. 'Well,' he says softly, 'here's your twelve blokes, now what?'

'Now,' the bloke says, 'they each have to put in half their tobacco ration.'

He waits until they do that under Robbi's direction. 'Right, now I take half of the amount and go out. That leaves half in the kitty, which we divide into two portions.' He does this and gives me one lot and Robbi the other. 'Now the pyramid splits into two, and when each pyramid gets made up into fifteen blokes, you both go out and then the pyramid splits again, and you've got four, but by then you're out of it with the loot, just as I am now.'

Robbi nods and I look at him. He's getting an idea from this game. His body's inflating in front of my eyes. He's regaining control of himself. He sends those in the pryamids out to grab blokes and then we're out of it. By then everyone wants to get into the act, and it goes on, until there isn't enough blokes left and the last pyramids collapse with mutual accusations all around; but by then Dick is out of it, though some of the New Block blokes are still in. They aren't that concerned, for Robbi's generous when it comes to giving people a smoke.

It's lock-up time and we line up to go back to our block and cells. 'That's it, that's simple and easy for people to understand,' Robbi remarks as we enter our cell, his voice already losing that hollowness. He takes out a sheet of paper and begins working something out. A diagram, or plan. I'm glad for him, because he's been such a drag over the last few years, months, days, weeks, eternities. It's good to see him back on the track; but what has he seen that I haven't seen?'

The Chief Screw ventures in that night and Robbi gets

into a long whispered conversation with him. The screw also is happy to see that his mate is back from the deeps; but he shakes his head at what Robbi is proposing, nods, then shakes his head again. Robbi shows him some figures. The Chief Screw says: 'Let me think about it.' He leaves shaking his head again.

Robbi looks at me and smiles: 'He'll come round. Now I'm hungry.' I get up and fix him some bread and jam, and watch him scoff it down. I can see his body inflating. The horrible depression is over. Things are looking up again already. I sit down and do my meditation on the forehead. There's not the slightest scream in my head. It's as clear as the blue sky over the sea, and the image brings back memories and I think of the outside. One of these days, I'll get out—but when?

9

Visiting

I've got this job to do for Robbi and I'm having trouble with it. We've got all this old machinery. Really, just bits and pieces. A couple of old flat board printers and a few other odds and ends that must've come from the Government Printers when they were having an update. What I need is a linotype, or something like that. Well, with a bit of luck, he'll have a reasonable job. It's that diagram he was working on the other night. I'm trying to composit that.

Well, I've just got it stacked up about right, when the shop screw comes towards me. I get to my feet to hide the block with my body and he tells me that I've got a visitor. A visitor, for me? After all these days and nights and months and weeks, someone has actually remembered me. I shrug and follow him to the print shop door.

One thing about boob is that you're never alone. Always got company and often of the unwelcome sort. You either go in a mob, or you get a screw to show you the way. So now he shows me the way towards the meeting place near the inner gate. Wish I could imagine myself doing something smart now and getting through that gate and out through the big, old, outer doors and down the street and into the town; but there's that job to do for Robbi which I realise I haven't covered up. If there is some sort of inspection and some screw points at it and says, 'What's that?' I might be in the shit, though I doubt it, for it's all backwards and a diagram and what screw could understand that?

We reach the place where I haven't been once, though

I've watched other cons come back from there with sour looks on their faces and sadness in their hearts. It's then that they get into blues and beat or get beaten with a savage intensity that shows they want to hurt, or be hurt. One or the other—it didn't matter. So having a visitor isn't that much fun. I wait for the screw to open the door and he gestures me inside, orders me to wait, then locks the door. He stands just inside and gestures me to meet my visitor. I go to the place where this woman is sitting and sit opposite her. There's a gap between us and we can't reach out and touch. Then there's this sort of scruffling noise and a little face pushes up beside her and a little hand starts pulling at her dress and this tiny voice says, 'Mummy, how long do we have to stay here?'

'Hush darling,' she replies, then ups her eyes to look at me.

I look back at her and blink. It's Denise, the doll of my dreams, the chick of my days, the one who loved me true. Oh, fuck! I stare at this, this apparition, and say, 'So, you're a mummy now?'

'It's yours,' she says. 'Brought him along so that you could see him.'

'You took your time,' I reply, for the kid is about four and that means I've been in here for that long. Ye gods, six years and more to go.

If I measured that length of time, I'd go crazy. Now it hits me. I realise that outside time isn't standing still. It's moving and taking people along with it. Once this girl/woman in front of me was a swinging chick at the milkbar. I remember her as a tough little moll, a swinging doll of seventeen out on the streets and hanging in there strong. She meets Wildcat then and we click. We make it a few times and she holds my hand as the blues hit and even then I can see, feel that gap in my life which is now. So, I look at her and the gap is a chasm. I look at the kid and I don't know the kid. I see the world in them and that world is moving from me and maybe it's for the better, for Denise looks done in by that world. She has on this old dress and her hair is sorta just pushed back and there is this, this harassed look on her dial. I stare at the kid and he is a mumma's boy and ignores me as he paws at her tit.

'Long time no see,' I say to say something.

She looks at me across the chasm. 'I just, just had to bring him so that you could see him.'

I try to think of the things you say in such circumstances. 'Yeah, he's got my eyes,' I reply, trying for a smile and just not making it. It's just too much. I've never ever thought in my wildest dreams that I would be a daddy, and now that I'm one, I have to reach for emotions I don't feel.

'And how're you getting on?' I ask.

'Well, there's the family,' she answers. 'They help out. I get by.'

I look at her and she looks away. 'It must've happpened that time after the milkbar when we had the wine and pills,' I say, trying for reminiscences. It doesn't work. She looks at me and I look away. I look at her and she looks away. I think of that bit of printing waiting for me to finish. I think of Robbi and what he would do in this situation. For the love of Christ, I don't know how to behave. Can't even pick up the kid, touch him, or his mum. There's this physical gap between us; there's this mental gap, and there's this time gap. There's even a Beckett gap. His 'I can't go on; I must go on' shit; but what is going on, or not going on? What has any of this got to do with me?

'He looks healthy,' I say.

'Never had a day's sickness in his life,' she replies proudly.

'Just like his dad,' and I can't help the sneer. Perhaps for this occasion, I should make up a poem. I can't think of anything else to do. I don't even feel happy, or sad, just, just untouched.

'Just wanted you to see him,' she says, repeating herself.

'I'm glad that you brought him along,' I reply, trying to remember how close I had been to this woman. How we didn't bug each other. How we shared a few good and bad scenes—and the result has been this kid.

'I don't believe it,' I say with an attempt at a smile.

'If you were outside, he might settle you down,' she replies, somehow imagining a future I can't.

'Might at that I say,' suddenly thinking that this might help me to get outside. I know for certain that it'll get on my file, and as Robbi says what's on your file you make use of. And then it's over. The screw orders me up and Denise and my, my son stand there looking after me as the screw unlocks the door. As I go through, I hear him say, 'Mummy, who was that man?' It is then that I remember that I didn't even ask his name.

So much for fatherhood, so much for visitors. I'm feeling like shit now. There's all that movement out there and in here I'm motionless. Life goes on, but not for me. I march along with the screw to the printing shop, just in time to pick up the mob and march to the cell block. We're going to be locked in for the night. We're going to be gnawing at our stale bread soon. Life is one big drag, man . . .

I get through the evening on no gear, and am glad to be in my bunk with the grid of the window marking out the night. I stare at it. No way out, and fall into a doze. My old uncle appears to me along with Mum. We're sitting in that kitchen of long ago, eating some stew. I gobble it down, and then my uncle farts and I'm in that forest of statues, creeping about at the foot of the pedestals. Crow lands on one of the heads and gives a squawk. I flutter up to him. He swoops off and lands on the ground. I follow and then along comes a little black and white bird with a twitching tail, a jitta-jitta, and he whispers to me and I fluttter off alongside him, feeling somewhat clumsy. He flutters about the heads and so do I, then the moon appears and I leave him and try to rise. My wings begin to fail. I begin falling. Wagtail flutters around anxiously, and the ground rises up. I come outa my doze to find that I've had a wet dream. I lie there looking at the grid, feeling that

I should be happy that I've managed to get off the ground; but all that I feel is a sense of loss. Why, I dunno. Maybe, one time, I'll really take off and rise above it all, rise not above stupid statues, but everything, and then I'll be joyous and free.

THE PANOPTICON

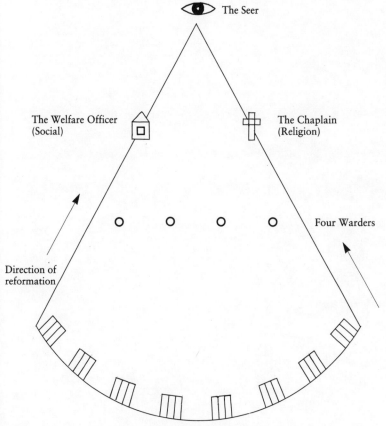

The Seer

The Welfare Officer
(Social)

The Chaplain
(Religion)

Four Warders

Direction of
reformation

Eight cells containing the eight seen

The Panopticon Prison Reform Society

We all know that there is a crying need not only to reform the prison system, but society in general. To do this, our society needs to have a means of raising funds. Our committee has devised the following plan to raise funds: Seers are requested to donate 10 per cent of their winnings to the Panopticon Society. We stress that this is not a game of chance, but a scientific means of circulating Wealth. The principles date from the Age of Enlightenment and the great economist, Adam Smith. It is to your advantage to participate in this economic plan of reform. You will get:

1 An opportunity to earn 1200 pounds within ten meetings

2 Members and visitors earn this by purchasing a cell for 150 pounds

3 We enter the plan by helping to reform 'prisoners', by bringing them into the Panopticon which holds fifteen people—a Seer, a Welfare Officer, a Chaplain, four Warders and eight Convicts

4 As Convicts keep on entering the Panopticon in which you are incarcerated, individually you keep on moving up, or being reformed until you become the Seer of your own Panopticon and collect your 1200 pounds as follows:

  a After you are fined and 'sentenced' you must inform on at least one (or more) criminals to fill up the empty cells b Once all eight cells (in the Panopticon in which you are incarcerated) have been filled, the original Seer collects the fines and is free

c As your original Seer exits, the Panopticon splits in half, becoming two separate prisons in which all people incarcerated (including you) are reformed, that is move up to Warders, Welfare Officer, Chaplain and Seer. The Welfare Officer and Chaplain respectively become Seers of their own Panopticon; the former Warders become Welfare Officer and Chaplain, and the former Convicts (now reformed) become Warders. Eight empty cells now must be filled in the new Panopticon

5 This process of incarceration and being reformed continues until you attain the position of Seer of your own completed Panopticon and become free

RULES

1 You must PAY THE FINE to enter the plan

2 You must be represented or ATTEND EVERY MEETING until you attain freedom

3 You must ESCORT IN AT LEAST ONE NEW CONVICT in order to remain a Welfare Officer or Chaplain and move from one of these positions to Seer to avoid being resentenced. Being resentenced means that you become a repeat offender and are returned to a cell, for failure to find one new offender

4 After being resentenced three times, you may be released by fining a new Convict 150 pounds and leaving the Panopticon

5 All moneys must be paid to, or received from the Treasurer of The Panopticon Prison Reform Society, or if he is not able to be in attendance, from the society member designated.

DISCIPLINES FOR REFORM AND FREEDOM

1 Think positively and strive to help those above you, reform those below you and cooperate with those beside you to

attain freedom and your economic reward won by your own efforts. Remember by your contribution you are not only reforming the prison system but also the state, thus ensuring prosperity to all

2 Be 'sentenced' quickly and enter your cell, then bring in others to be reformed. The faster you rise, the sooner you shall attain your freedom

3 Use our meetings as opportunities to organise and network with the people who will be reforming your particular Panopticon and whose participation will ensure your rise to freedom

4 Bring new people to meetings so that they may develop an interest in our work

5 Devote your time only to developing an attitude that will ensure your rise to freedom. Focus on the goal, and the economic reward. Please, we urge you to donate 10 per cent of your earnings to our Worthy Cause. Membership of our society is open to all those who believe in reform, freedom and prosperity. If you develop the correct attitude it may be possible for you to participate in the Corporate Panopticon which describes not the imperfect prison segment, but the perfect social circle which in turn maps out a complete economic system for the circulation of Wealth. For a prosperous and healthy Western Australia you are invited to participate in and further the aims of our society.

2

Reformation

In the lower hall of the Fremantle Town Hall, 30 people sit in straight-backed chairs waiting for the ecomonic plan to be put into operation. In front of them, on a platform, are three empty chairs. Below these is a segment of four empty chairs. These face eight others. A keen observer notes that the chairs are close enough to cause the discomfort of eye contact, but still at a distance far enough from each other to reduce this discomfort to some degree. The chairs are precisely arranged so that they form the sector of a circle with the apex being the chair in the centre of the platform.

The quite large audience, that is for Fremantle, stirs as three men enter the hall from the back and move along the side aisle towards the platform. One of them is obviously an ex-army man. He has the bearing of a British officer and is adorned with a military moustache; the other is somehow, that is at present, not to their liking. Apart from his bulk (which less compassionate people might term obesity) there is the brown colour of his skin which, as most of these people are of British stock, shows him to be a foreigner and what's more a wog of some sort. It is little wonder that they are somewhat dismayed when he, and not the fine-looking ex-army officer, takes the central chair—but then this is a charity do, and he must be an object of charity. Thus, the members of the audience are both quick to indulge their prejudices but just as quick are they to overcome these very prejudices when the object of their disquiet can be perceived as a victim, and therefore comfortably assigned

to a lower level in the scheme of things. The third man
most of them hesitate over. Some might recognise in the
cold eyes and upright position, the posture of a private soldier.
The majority put him down as a police officer or prison
warder. They carefully avoid his cold eyes which sweep over
them, rendering them into so many objects, or disposable
items, or even vicitms.

A fourth man, a grey person of no obvious charm, enters
to distribute to each of them three sheets of paper. Two
contain diagrams and the third is a list of rules. As they
have been there for some time, they read over the sheets,
some recognising from the correspondence they have entered
into with this prison reform society that the diagrams appear
to refer to what else but prison reform. As yet, they cannot
make head or tail out of the rules of the economic plan;
but they all realise that money may be made from it. The
grey person finishes handing out the sheets. He goes and
sits in the first of the four chairs in the body of the hall
facing the audience. His eyes do not disconcert them. All
in all they recognise a placid man, one of their own kind.

They relax thinking about the 1200 pounds.

The military man gets to his feet and stands at attention.
His eyes sweep the audience. He begins in an authoritative
voice:

'The Panopticon Prison Reform Society until now has
been only a matter of correspondence between you good people
and us, the organisers, who are experts in the penal system.
Every day, we see the sad results of a prison system which
is not functioning as it should. It must be reformed. My
colleagues and I feel that now is the time to broaden the
base of our appeal, to bring this worthy cause to the notice
of the general public. In order to do this, we must have
a program which is readily understandable, scientific and
practical. It is not enough to expose the abuses and
delinquencies of the present system, more must be done. A
systematic plan of reform must be presented, and more and
more people must be made aware of our, shall I say,

movement, and to do this we must have funds. A movement without funding is as powerless as a convict in his lonely cell, and I know all of you realise this. Now with this short introduction concluded, I wish to call on the founder of our movement, an old soldier as I am myself, to address you.'

The rather stout, coloured man, for they are polite people and would not use the terms 'fat' or 'wog' consciously, gets to his feet, and his bulk overawes them. Some fat men have a reedy voice which shrills out to make them figures of compassion; but this man doesn't. His voice is deep and sonorous and filled with compassion. They forget his bulk in the play of his voice.

'Our chief aim is to further this humane and most worthy movement. Through correspondence we have been able to spread the word and collect enough donations to rent this hall. Ladies and gentlemen it is only a beginning; but if there is to be an end result we must have a beginning and further we must have the means to continue our work. Perhaps you are thinking, but what shall we, you or I get from this society? It is not enough to have meetings and listen to people such as myself drone on about prison reform, and even social reform, for the prison is but the central aspect of society. One which permeates everything. We must come to some understanding of this, and to do that we, each of us, must participate. We are all Children of the Enlightenment, of the Age of Adam Smith, the famous economist, and of Jeremy Bentham, the philosopher who stated that the aim of society is to give the greatest happiness to the greatest number. He it was who bequeathed to us the name of our society "The Panopticon," and who began the first movement in modern prison reform. It was he, also, who gave us the rational economic system inherent in the diagram before you. Adam Smith needs no introduction. A Professor of Moral Philosophy at Glasgow University, he espoused Bentham's principles and shared with him a common interest in the progress of the science of economics. Both were great humanists and enlightened thinkers. Both shared a common vision, a vision which they encoded in the diagram before you. It contains sound economic principles which will not only benefit you, but all society.

'Now, you may ask, what has this to do with prison reform? It is a matter of common knowledge that both philosophers were at the forefront of not only prison reform, but economic reform. They wished for the happiness of the majority, for when the happiness of the majority is assured, then so is the happiness of the minority. The way to happiness, of economic and social prosperity, is reached by passing through the Panopticon as encoded in the diagram.

'This Panopticon and the system of prosperity encoded within it, I declare, without hesitation, shall be the model for the kind of economy we shall be having in Western Australia in twenty years or so. Those who enter the Panopticon and pass into freedom find themselves at the leading edge of humanity. They have learnt a system which will not only ensure their own prosperity, but that of their beautiful state as well. When individuals are happy and prosperous so is their social system. I stress that it is impossible to lose in this system of enrichment.

'The Panopticon is about self-empowerment, is about leaving the prison of ourselves to advance into prosperity. In entering it you shall learn about yourself, about your own life, and how to further your ambitions and interests. Not only this, but through entering into the Panopticon you shall not only be helping yourself, but aiding our and your society in its aim of prison reform. Prison reform rests on activating the Panopticon, and to do this we must have funds. Thus, we urge you when you enter the Panopticon and pass through into freedom, that you give 10 per cent of your reward to our cause. I do not wish to belabour the point, or to sway you by mere words. I have said enough about our prosperity system. To see how it works for you, you must enter and pass through. I myself and my two colleagues are ready to begin. We shall break for refreshments and discussion, and then begin the first economic plan. I trust that it is the first of many, and at this point in our growth, I can only allude to what is termed the Corporate Panopticon, Adam Smith and Jeremy Bentham's geatest discovery, when the eight segments of the encoded diagram join together into the perfect circle of the perfect society to form the perfect company. If you wish to learn more about this, please see Mr Reading, our treasurer. I may say here that participation in this leads to an eight-fold increase in your reward. Now please study your diagram, talk it over with us at the break, and decide. Perhaps you shall go on to complete the perfect circle of the perfect company, at the very centre of which is placed the Great Architect of the Age of Enlightenment. It is this Corporate Director who gives us everlasting prosperity. Thank you, ladies and gentlemen for listening to me.'

The ladies and gentlemen are quite taken in by the address of Subedhar Robbi Singh and his colleague whom, they quickly learn is not only a war hero, but the Chief Warder of the nearby state prison, and thus above reproach. The Panopticon Prison Reform Society thus has official sanction and so many decide to enter into the Panopticon. It may be interpolated here that it is from this meeting that the temporary prosperity and eventual economic collapse of Western Australia began, together with the subsequent scandals which rocked the entire political and economic system of the state. It is only now that Robbi Singh's place in the annals of Western Australia may be exposed without the threat of legal action. Perhaps it should be seen as only fair and just that the new maximum security prison replacing the old State Prison in Fremantle should bear his name. The state owes him an undying debt of gratitude, and I may end this interpolation with the information that he was not only the author of the epithet, 'The State of Excitement,' but was instrumental in aiding that euphoric state by bringing to Western Australia a cherished international trophy, as well as ensuring that the famed casino came into being under the most proper ownership. He shall not be forgotten.

3

The Corporate Panopticon

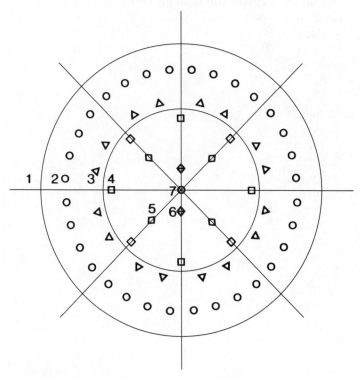

1. Outer circle: 8 segments;
   8 Shareholders per segment,
   64 total Shareholders
2. 4 Company Managers per segment:
   total 32 Company Managers
3. 16 General Managers:
   2 per segment

4. 8 Directors
5. 4 Board Members
6. 2 Vice-Presidents
7. President or Corporate Director

Possible Earnings £9,600/-

SURVEILLANCE

1

The Law

Detective Watson Holmes Jackamara looks askance at the oldish, well-groomed man in the tweed suit sitting at the desk. Jackamara stands at attention supposedly with his eyes straight ahead; but he is an army veteran and has the ability to see what he wants to see while seemingly his eyes are focussed straight ahead. Such abilities or skills enable the detective to keep ahead of things as he puts it. A man not known for boasting, he is remarkably quiet about his remarkable three months behind enemy lines during the Korean War which earns him a high military award and a field commission. But that's the past, and he wonders why he is recalling it while he stands at attention like a, like a copper in uniform. He shrugs slightly, a faint dipping of the shoulder which does not communicate itself to the man sitting stiffly behind his desk and ostensibly ignoring him.

The Commissioner of the Western Australian Police Force, he knows, is an ex-army man himself, a Colonel of the British Army and a strict disciplinarian. In fact, in his very short time in Western Australia, Jackamara has gained the impression that the state has the attributes of a British colony rather than a state of Australia, because it has been settled by refugees from the British Army and colonial administrations who migrated here from other British possessions which had gained independence after the Second World War.

The man raises steely-grey eyes to Jackamara's dark face and recalls his attention with a cough before speaking.

'Detective, ah, Watson Holmes Jackamara. It appears that your arrival was, or is timely. The prisoner you escorted fortunately was not the person we wanted. I say fortunately because a slight matter has arisen for which none of our chaps will do. It needs a stranger and one of, well, of your appearance and peculiar abilities. No one will suspect you, and your loyalty and discretion are unquestioned.'

'Yes, sir,' Jackamara agrees, wondering what he exactly is agreeing to.

'Come, come, man, you're not in the army now,' the Commissioner says jovially as if to put him at ease. 'Damn good job, that, eh? Showed natural ability, yes natural ability. A Gunga Din mentality. At ease. Sit down. I'll get some tea sent in. Good.'

He marches to the door, flings it open, barks for tea, does an about-turn and surveys the coloured chappie. He nods when he sees that the Aboriginal detective has obeyed his order to be seated and sits there quietly waiting to serve. Damn good, some of these native troops had been. He marches back to his own chair and sits upright there for a long moment. He leans forward and opens a file. From it he takes a number of sheets of paper and passes them across the desk to Jackamara. He opens his mouth, his lips form the words 'You can . . .' before he thinks better of it. He leans back, sternly waiting for the detective to look up. He does so and says: 'Well, sir . . . ?'

'I know it won't mean much to one of you, I mean to an average chap at all. What we are concerned about is that the diagrams and indeed the words themselves have been printed at the prison. The state's maximum security prison and how and why it was done there and what this, this Panopticon Prison Reform Society is, is not exactly unknown to us. Indeed, though you may find this hard to believe, the whole society has been set up from within the prison with active support and connivance by a senior officer in the penal service. If this was all, things might be simple— remove the bad apple and all that—but you see, well, this diagram I found with my wife. Never mind that. Not part of it at all. What I want to do is to get a man inside for a while; have him give the place an eye over; see what he can find out; you know what I mean . . .'

'Yes, sir,' Jackamara agrees, not liking the assignment at all. He might just run into one of the villains he has put away in Queensland and then blood could flow, though it is more than likely to be the villain's rather than his own. Still, that is one aspect he can handle, and he would be working on his own. He likes that; but working on his own behind high walls and in an environment where at least one of the authorities might be hostile is an entirely different matter. He stares at the Commissioner who, for all his army background, is thorough and would not be wittingly putting a policeman in danger.

'There's some problem in getting you in,' the Commissioner continues. 'You see the police and the penal service aren't on good terms at the best of times and now with a wrong'un amongst them, and not just any screw, er warder, if they knew you were coming it would be like giving you a guided tour of the place, eh what?'

'Yes, sir,' Jackamara sighs, wondering how the Colonel might solve the problem and if indeed it was true that he was looking out for his welfare, though he understands why he is being used. The state has a small population, and this reminds him.

'Beg pardon, sir,' he states. 'But I'm a member of the Queensland Police Force and thus have no authority in this state.' In reply the Commissioner thrusts a telegram towards him. Jackamara glances at it. He has been seconded to the Western Australian Police Force for a period at the Commissioner's discretion. 'A bit like a prison sentence,' the detective sighs. He has been looking forward to his leave which he was to have spent on his mission home. The Commissioner catches the sigh.

'I know you want to get home to, to your mangoes and bananas, to your little place under the sun; but you are needed for this little job. I and my personal secretary have worked on the details and contacted the necessary people. We think a week in the nick will be enough; then you're to be pulled out. All done through the legal system, no foul-ups that way. You'll be sentenced for, for embezzlement. You're a missionary chappie from up north. Came down here with your good Father fella to collect for his mission, couldn't help yourself, too many goodies in the city, so you put your hand in the collecting tray. Got caught, now sentenced. Judge throws the book at you and all that. Later, the good Father finds he's made a mistake in the adding up. Good Christian he comes to us, confesses his error and you're sprung. How'd you like it?' he says leaning back and beaming up at the detective.

'Well, sir,' the detective says, smiling wryly. Christ, these Migloos or as they called them over here Watjelas are tricky ones. 'Will it work, sir?' he asks, hoping that they won't forget him and leave him in for the duration of the sentence. He is, and he can't help being, apprehensive that this just might be a plot by the Queensland Police Force to get rid of him once and for all, and in a state where he is unknown. He has embarrassed the force on more than one occasion, and the current Police Commissioner there . . . well, it is unlikely. After all, he is the most decorated policeman in their force and a worthy token to be trotted out when accusations of racism are hurled . . .

'Of course, of course,' the Commissioner snaps. 'Simple operation. Piece of cake. Everything is settled. You are to report for sentencing tomorrow at the court building at ten. Just surrender to the policeman on duty and he'll take you down to the holding cell. The trial will be just a formality. The court has been apprised. If there is nothing further you wish to know, you are dismissed. Good luck and . . .'

'Yes, sir?'

'Good hunting.'

'Thank you, sir.'

Jackamara gets to his feet, represses a salute, does an

about-turn and marches out. He breathes a sigh of relief, for he finds these colonial types somewhat hard to take, or fathom. Good hunting indeed, when he was to be flung into prison where the only hunting most likely would be done by the warders. Christ, what an assignment. Why, he doesn't even know where the blasted prison is, or the court building for that matter. He's only been in the state for two days and doesn't know where anything is except police headquarters and his hotel. He shrugs, then smiles as he makes his way to the hotel room the police have booked him into. Simple police duties have never interested him. Only the unusual, and this case may have those ingredients which will satisfy his keen mind and thirst for adventure. He sits on the bed and plans the operation . . .

It is towards sunset and the sun shifts down into the harbour streaking long bars of light towards the high sandstone walls of the prison. The prison is to one side of the town centre and stands there, an immovable block around which all must circle, or enter. Not many of the port community enter, nor do they accept the warders as members of their community, although they have their quarters next to the prison. In fact, the population of the port has more in common with the prisoners who, when they are released, linger to roister in the lanes and narrow streets before departing from, or on many occasions, after a few days, returning to that prison on the hill dominating the skyline of the port.

So now the sun streaks light into and through those windows facing towards the sea, and if a convict is staring out with the necessary angle and arc of vision, he might see and be envious of the tall, heavy-set black man dressed in cowboy clothing lurching towards the prison gates. The man reaches the main gates and falls against them, curses and staggers away. The heavy wooden doors do not open. If someone wants to contact the gate warder, there is a bellpull to one side. It is rarely used this late in the day and only then when a warder has been unexpectedly rostered for a night shift.

The drunken Aboriginal stockman leaves the main gate. He staggers along the road which curves around the prison wall. Every now and again, he hesitates, sways, loses his balance and sits down with a thud. Each time, if there was an observer with the keen sight of a Watson Holmes Jackamara, he would note that such falls occur under a guard tower, or at a spot where some some sort of irregularity in the construction of the wall makes it theoretically scaleable, though he would know that the terrain within has been excavated and contours changed, making it difficult to determine whether it was as impregnable as it appeared from without. Finally, the drunk comes to a door cut within the wall. He lurches against it and as if in a drunken rage begins battering away with his fists. There is no response from inside, and the drunk slides down and into unconsciousness. It is then that such an observer would come to investigate; but there is no one and the man curls up out like a light against the door.

2

Incarcerated

The uniform shoves Jackamara into the holding cell below the court. 'Shut up,' he growls as if the detective has given him cheek, then reveals that he is in the know with a wink. 'God, they're all actors,' says the black man to himself as he stands, not knowing what to do. It is his first time on the other side, and he isn't finding it an enjoyable experience. The cell in which he finds himself is a small cage crowded with five prisoners. There are no chairs or benches, for a sentenced man often turns into a desperate man willing to turn to any weapon with which to batter his way to freedom. This Jackamara knows from experience; but from the outside, not from what will now be first-hand inner knowledge.

'You know,' says a bloke sidling up to him and studying him with furtive, wary eyes. Jackamara has arrested such eyes, but now he must try to be sympathetic to them. Thank God he is an Aborigine and thus different from such people. He is unaware that his keen glance around the cell when he entered has betrayed him. It reveals him not to be your average blackfella. He appears able to handle things; too much like a white man, and thus a troublemaker. *Giving himself airs*, the bloke thinks, as he grabs for the blackfella's attention. 'You know,' the bloke repeats, for he's just been on a fortnight's binge and his brain's not recovered. 'You know,' he says for a third time, while Jackamara is reeling from the stench of old grog and vomit and looking around the cell for an escape. He pushes past two men to reach the grille. He looks at the winding spiral of stairway ascending into the defendant's box. 'That's what I want to tell you about,' the bloke says, following after and clutching Jackamara's arm. 'See that spiral staircase, see where they've put wire mesh about it, you know why? There was this chap, he killed his wife, sawed her up, and mailed the bits to her mum, he did. Then he was sentenced to be hung and he was coming down those stairs when he grabbed the copper that was escorting him and both went to the ground with him on top. That copper never moved after that. His head all smashed in from the fall; but the other bloke not hurt at all, not a bruise on him, until after, when those coppers come and take him across to headquarters, take him there and he has a little accident, falls from a third-storey window, and he's lying there, more bruises on him than from any fall. That's what coppers are like, they is, mate, and they hate uppity boongs,' he snarls viciously and vindictively.

Detective Watson Holmes Jackamara assumes his Aboriginal stockman persona. He mumbles a few words and slinks to the wall. He is about to sink onto the floor when another bloke, an old white one, comes up to him and says: 'Another of your mob was with me not the last time, or the other time, but the time before that, or was it. He shot a copper. Wild darkie, that one. Young'un too. Too young for the army. You know, I was in the first boat to hit the beach at the Cove. First one off too. Bodies falling all around. Machine-guns crackling; fifteen pounders and what have you booming. Rifles falling outa blokes' hands as they dropped dead. A mess, mate, a mess. You ever been in a big one?'

'Korea,' Jackamara says abruptly, then recovers. 'Yeah,' he quickly adds. 'Those fellas camped up where I been herding these cows, you know for old MacMarah on the Danube. Up there, and these fellas, hundreds and hundreds of them. All with, you know, slouched hats, big boots. Not as good as me cowboy boots; too heavy for that. Have to carry 'em when you walking, heavy as that. And guns. They had big guns, little guns, this size guns and that size guns. Got a bit of drink from them one time, and I ask them, "Eh, you going to a war or somethin', just like I seen in the pictures?" And they didn't think it funny, 'cause they were going to a war, like that John Wayne fought. Like him better in those cowboy flicks though. This shirt just like the one he wore in, can't think of the name now. John Wayne, soldier just like you. Yeah, old Anzac, eh? You march each year, eh?'

The old codger stares at Jackamara and begins mumbling about being the first to land at Gallipoli again. Thankfully, just then his name is called and he is taken away. The detective is beginning to realise that being imprisoned is being locked up with others you cannot escape from—but for now he has. Up that spiral staircase he goes to come out before the judge. Now he knows what it is like to be in the dock. He stares across at the judge, and feels that person deliberately ignoring him. He is of no concern or consequence. Only another felon to be sentenced. He is asked to plea. Suddenly, it is not just an arrangement with justice he is acting out; but a reality in which he will be sentenced to a term in Her Majesty's prison. He hesitates over the plea as if he has a choice. He definitely is 'not guilty'; but will that mean anything? Law is not based on the word of the defendant; but on the presentation of evidence before a bewigged, self-righteous man who will determine whether the defendant is innocent, or guilty, and then he will weigh up whatever he weighs up to determine the gravity of the crime, mitigating circumstances and other intangibles, and then too often it's boob for you, my man, it's boob for you.

So Jackamara looks down and around the court where no one is taking the slightest notice of him. So much for being a criminal, he thinks, then the judge turns on him a reddened eye and snarls: 'Well, get on with it, plea, can't you, plea.' And so Jackamara says 'guilty', and the judge is satisfied and gives him what appears to be a smile of complicity, and suddenly it is all make-believe and he is relieved; for just one minute, or two, or three he has felt himself on the other side of the law. A felon waiting to be justly sentenced and with the feeling of the bars moving in to enclose him. Now, secure in his belonging, in being part of the due process of law, he waits, while the judge shuffles some papers, coughs, and then declares: 'To rob one's master is a crime which threatens society; to rob not only one's master, but his and your holy church is a crime almost beyond forgiveness. I have taken your race and your lack of the pleasing balms of civilisation into account, still, you have been taught well, and know the difference between right and wrong, thus I sentence you to five years' hard labour.' And he hits his gavel, and the policeman beside Jackamara touches his elbow and whispers: 'Bet you'd be shitting yourself, if that was what you had to serve, eh?'

Jackamara nods, but does not return the police constable's smile. Already there seems too many people in the know, and that spells trouble when you have to operate undercover. He is pushed back into the cell, where the slimy bloke who first talked to him, sidles over to ask: 'How much?'

'Five years,' Jackamara replies.

'Blimey, the world'll be a different place by the time you see it again, Jacky,' he smirks, gloating for some reason Jackamara can't ascertain.

'Could do it on my head,' the old army codger says. 'Been in the army, you can stand anything after that. Anything! I was on the first boat to land at the Cove. First one out too,' and on he goes and Jackamara switches off.

Then the copper unlocks the door and growls: 'All right, you lot, out to the van. Look lively now.'

They march into a small exercise yard where a van is backed up to the exit. They get in and the door clangs and for the first time Jackamara feels the walls closing in and the outside separating itself from him. A convicted felon. Locked up with other convicted felons. Inside the van the others look at one another, or try to peer into another's eyes for support, while seeking a few last glimpses of freedom through the close meshes of the side windows. Flashes of, of a void. The outside recedes from him. He who loves the wide-open spaces and freedom is going to be locked up for, thank God, only a week. He breathes easily, as the old codger has stated: 'He can do that standing on his head.'

The prison gates open wide; the inner grille is unlocked and the van rolls through to the other side of the law. Jackamara and the other prisoners get out and are ordered to stand in a line. They are escorted into the reception centre at the side of the shower block. The screw inside stares at them with a cold look which tells Jackamara that he has arrived and is truly in the shit. Well, and he grins, thinking that a policeman's lot is not a happy one. 'Wipe that grin off your face,' the screw yells. 'You ain't in no bloody holiday camp. Get them clothes off, fold them to go with your other personal possessions.'

The warders stare at the prisoners as they disrobe. They eye them with a cold disgust which is worse than any desire, for it renders the bodies impersonal, so much cattle to be penned. Jackamara himself does his own looking; and his gaze is just as impersonal. The bodies of the other men are flabby and out of condition, whereas, although he has put on a bit of flesh around the middle, he is dark and this seems to make him feel less naked than the others. He even lightly punches his stomach testing the flab. His retaining of his humanity is out of character.

A warder's gaze suddenly turns sentient. A person out of character. He knows his cons and how they react to the bars, to the treatment. This bloke is either a troublemaker, or one of those idiots who can be happy in a zoo. As he is a boong, he most likely is of the latter type and wouldn't cause any trouble to the warders at least. His gaze returns as he dismisses him and the others. Just the usual lot of no-hopers. Petty crims without a brain amongst the lot . . .

'Right,' he yells, 'you skinned lot come to the counter one by one. Place your clothes there and sign in your personal property . . . Come on, step on it.' Jackamara asks to check his personal possessions. The warder up-ends the large brown envelope, scoops the things back inside, snarls 'Satisfied?' and then thrusts a pen in his hand. 'Just a cross will do, Jacky,' he sneers. Jackamara refuses to be taunted. In fact, he is relieved to be accepted at face value. He signs with a cross, and the screw laughs and throws the envelope to a trustee who tosses it onto a shelf. Jackamara steps back and waits, and waits. Just like the army, he realises, or a police parade, or action. Everything to be done together and by the order. At last, the next step is entered into. A perfunctory examination by a doctor. Naked they pass before him to be prodded and checked, then are escorted into showers where under the gaze of a bored warder, they scrub their bodies with an evil-smelling soap. The dirt is replaced by a thin screen of grease which gives them that peculiar jail smell that permeates the atmosphere. If smells could have colours, the colour of this smell would be grey, thinks Jackamara wondering how his dog would recognise him now. A couple of convicts bring in baskets of clothing which they plonk down. Each man is ordered to parade past and receive in appropriate sizes and rough cuts of a strange rough hessian material, a coat, a pair of trousers, a collarless shirt and flannel undershirt, and a pair of shoes with a buckle at the side. All are shapeless and grey.

'Just like the army,' the old codger whispers as he pulls on his shapeless garments. 'Have to put up with this lot for the next week until we go to the clothing store to get some clean ones. You'll get a better fit then if you give the blokes there a couple of smokes.'

'Urrh,' replies Jackamara, neither agreeing nor disagreeing. The master of disguise is not happy with his appearance. He seems more a derelict than when he has dressed as a derelict. All in all, it is perfect. He doesn't even feel like a detective let alone look like one.

They are huddled waiting for the order which will escort them elsewhere when the telephone, an old-fashioned one with the earpiece separate, rings. The screw picks up the ear piece and growls into the mouthpiece poking out from the square wooden box of the instrument case. He agrees a few times with a nodding of his head, grunts, then replaces the instrument on its hook, twirls the little handle to ring off, then eyes the convicts until they look either away or at the ground. 'Now you lot, let's hope you're as clean as daisies. We've a Black Peter for those caught smuggling contraband in.'

He goes to a door facing eastwards into the prison, and unlocks it with a great jangling of keys. He heaves the door open and waits for those convicts who have brought the clothing to come out with their baskets, then orders the others out. He lines them up and marches them towards the clothing store to cast off the clothing cons, then wheels his troop towards the administrative block.

In the guard box on top of the wall, the bored warder moves out onto the platform and stares down at the marching convicts. A new lot, but why are they making directly for the admin block instead of going to the main division? Then he sees the Superintendent come out of the block and stop beside the rose garden outside the door. He makes a show of bending over and examining the blooms of which he is inordinately proud. It doesn't pay to be proud of anything in prison, for the warder as he leans over can still make out the damage inflicted by a group of cons under the order of a warder backed up by a few ounces of tobacco. The screw smiles as he remembers how the Super had run out to save his precious plants. Well, what did he expect, trying to act as if he ran the prison, when they all knew that if it wasn't for the Chief Warder there would be chaos? The Chief was an all right bloke; but as for the Super with his tit-for-tat reports which go against a man for all of his working career, the best that could be said for him was that when he retired in two years that wouldn't be soon enough for them. He stares down at his fellow officer ordering the new convicts to come to a halt near the Superintendent. This is out of prison routine, but the warder on the wall knows that it is just another attempt by the Super to stick his beak in where it isn't wanted. It is then that the Super glances towards the tower. The guard instantly picks up his weapon, an old Lee Enfield and looks alert.

The Superintendent lifts his hooked nose from a large Western Beauty Rose, flicks his eyes up at the guard box to see if the man there is alert, then acknowledges the line of convicts. He stares particularly at Clarrie, the old digger who has become a fixture in the place. A pervert whom he will long remember. Once when he was escorting a party of ladies around the flower gardens which were his contribution to prisoner welfare and well-being, the man had had the temerity to flash his wizened dick at them. The ladies were too shocked to admire his flowers and had to leave instantly. The old pervert received a bigger shock later when he had been sentenced to twenty-eight days in the Black Peter. If it was possible he would have given him more, or better yet sent him off to the asylum in Claremont; but although the man was obviously insane and in need of treatment, the mental authorities had refused to even examine him, preferring to regard it as a plot by the prison authorities to get rid of a troublesome convict. He sighs as he looks at the gaps in his rose garden, and sighs again for the very idea of a plot brings up the lack of cooperation, in fact on occasion downright insubordination, on the part of his men which threatens the smooth running of his institution and overall discipline. Too many of them ex-army men, unable to take orders from a civilian. But how to change it when only these were willing to accept the hardships of the penal service? Thank God he has the friendship of the Chief Warder. A war hero who manages to keep things running. Without him, there might be outright mutiny. It was only a matter of time, for their grievances about pay and working conditions must come to a head sometime; and worst of all his men blame him. They have no understanding of the way things are ordered. If the Minister ignores his reports, well there is nothing he can do about it. Now to cap it all, they, that is the police, have got it into their heads that there is some sort of problem involving the convicts in the New Block, and even rumours of convicts being seen outside. Absurd! Someone, he is sure, is undermining his position. Now he has to go along with some sort of undercover investigation in his own prison. Nothing will come of it, he is sure. He glances along the line and meets the eyes of Jackamara. Only a police man would dare meet his eyes; but why a blackfellow of all people? Now he is to be assigned to the New Block under absolute secrecy. No one, not even the Chief Warder is to be informed. Well, a simple enough matter. Order the warder there to take him along to the block and that will be that. He darts a glance up at the guard box and sees the guard there leaning down and surveying the scene. He turns his eyes down and above him the warder spits, yawns and surreptitiously lights up a cigarette. 'All quiet on the Western Front.'

3

The Carceral

A feeling steals up from Jackamara's kidneys. A grey emotion of depression. The harsh clothing abrades his skin. His eyes flee out only to come up against the carceral formations of walls. Everywhere, everywhere a penning in. His free spirit rebels against it; but rebellion comes up against all-seeing eyes and those eyes join other eyes . . . Under surveillance, always under surveillance; but then hasn't he always been, he questions in order to re-establish the rationality of his keen mind. Eyes marking him out, tagging and following him from that first missionary Father to the police college, to the sergeant in the police station, to the eyes in the street which glide across him, his body and classify it and with it himself. And this, this universal watching holds sway in this place. Incarcerated, locked up, and like many cons he declares an innocence which means nothing. He has been judged, found guilty and locked up. Guilty, whether he likes it or not, for he knows how he reacts when a suspect declares his innocence. He laughs, or smiles ruefully as he snaps the cuffs about the criminal's wrists. Until now, he has never placed himself in the place of the victim. No, not the victim, but the criminal and where he hopes to send him. Now he is among them, now he is in that place. Now he is having the same experience as these felons, though he is, is not a delinquent, is not a crim, and will be out in a week. Thank God for that, but still that grey mist fills his body and head and world. He struggles to push it away and formulate some plan of action. He has to keep his eyes and ears open. He, the investigator, is part of those all-seeing eyes and must observe all impartially . . . He regains strength from his authority. He is part of the seer, not the seen.

'Right youse, stop there.' The screw opens the door leading into the main division. 'Right youse, inside.'

The warder passes the group over to the division screws together with their files. As it is the main division there are always a number of screws on duty, and it is an easy matter to get the new men into cells, each one clasping his ration of a quarter of a loaf of bread. Later, when the other convicts return from work, they'll get a mug of tea, but until then they're left to contemplate their living quarters.

Jackamara has been left to his own devices until the end. His own devices means that he has been left standing in front of the office whil the others have been taken care of. When they have been settled, one of the screws comes to him with his file and looks down at it: 'So the Super wants you in the New Block, eh? Dunno why, most of you boongs are happy enough in the second division. You ex-army? Must be, they don't want anyone else in there.'

Jackamara nods, and the screw takes offence. 'Well, is it "yes", or "no"? Got a mouth haven't you? Any more of this dumb insolence and I'll have you up on a charge. A few days in the Black Peter'll get you cooperating.'

Detective Watson Holmes Jackamara is used to discipline from the mission, the police force and the army. He shifts into that mode and says smartly: 'Yes, sir, Korea.'

The screw relaxes. 'Well, that's better, though I didn't know they took boongs. Still, expect you lot can make good fighters. Black and a private of course. Well, a lot of us are army in here and we want to run a tight unit. So just remember your old training and you'll be all right. You'll settle in, especially in New Block where the blokes look after their own. They couldn't hack it in civvy street and feel right at home here.'

'Right, sir,' Jackamara barks in his best army/police voice. He might have saluted, but being in mufti it is uncalled for.

'Well, let's get you to your new barracks,' and the screw marches him to the end of the division where a barred door confronts him. Jackamara watches closely as the warder opens the door, then marches him through, locks the door behind them, orders him to halt, and then pulls a bell lead which causes another screw to come and open a second grille door. He orders Jackamara through, says a few words to the main division warder, accepts the file, then both screws re-enter their divisions and carefully lock the doors behind them.

The warder in charge of the New Block is friendlier than the other ones through whose hands Jackamara has passed. He even smiles as he strolls to his office without ordering him to follow. 'Come on,' he says, when he sees Jackamara standing at attention at the very same place which is just a step inside the door into the New Block. 'We're more relaxed here, you know. All army chaps and all that. I say you're not a ring-in are you?'

Jackamara comes towards the office: 'Korea, United Nations.'

'And . . . ?'

'Private.'

'Well, I suppose we all can't reach the top. We seem to have a problem on our hands. We're a bit short of cells. Well, we'll just have to see what we can do, won't we, eh, private?'

Jackamara has received a field commission to Lieutenant. He feels that the warder might have detected the officer residing above the private, and he is a detective. He breathes easily as the man ignores him to begin studying his chart of cells. Jackamara examines the New Block while he waits. What he can see of it. He stares through an open cell door through which he sees shelves of books. The doorway becomes blocked by a fat brown man placing one rather dainty foot on the end of a huge barrel of a leg over the door sill. He heaves the block of his body over and comes waddling towards them.

'Robbi Singh,' he informs Jackamara, poking out his huge

paw and grabbing his fingers in a grip which threatens to break them before it relaxes. The man's dark eyes move over Jackamara examining every minute detail and then fasten on his face. He seems very interested in him and Jackamara can't understand why. 'Army?' he says. Jackamara nods. 'Can see it in you,' the fat man replies, then asks: 'What are you in for?'

This is a question which Jackamara has decided to tackle in a somewhat traditional fashion. 'Well, this bloke said that I took this money. Religious bloke too, worked for him I did, but he took me along to the police station and charged me. I wouldn't steal from the church. Not me, mate, not me.'

'No, not you. And how is Broome these days?' the fat man queries. Not waiting for an answer, he waddles across to the warder and places one familiar hand on his shoulder: 'If it is all right with you, I'll take this new chum into the library for a cup of tea. There's an hour or two before the cell muster and what will he be doing until then but moping in his cell? I was up his way once and am interested in how things are these days. Perhaps we have, have mates in common.'

The warder grunts, then protests: 'There's only a corner cell available. They're so small that I wouldn't put a dog in them; but for the moment, it'll have to do. As soon as one of the other blokes is released I'll move you. Now go and have your tea with Singh.'

Jackamara enters the library to find another convict there. Instantly, he is on guard. He knows the type. What he might call a vicious animal, unless held in check. And he sees that the man doesn't like him either. Suspiciously, they keep their distance.

Robbi says, 'This is, is . . . ?'

'Johnny Watson,' Jackamara informs them, 'sometimes known as Doc.'

'You look like some sorta copper,' the young bloke snarls.

'Yeah, I got flat feet,' Jackamara says, attempting a joke at which the wirehead scowls.

'This is Dick, my, my bodyguard,' Robbi Singh says, stepping in to lessen the animosity. 'You see, we have quite a good set-up here. We maintain the discipline; make sure that there are no problems or disturbances and so the warders are careful not to upset the applecart. Of course, sometimes there are problems from new blokes like yourself. If there is, the bloke is transferred from the division. It is as simple as that. Still, I know that you won't cause trouble. I'm looking forward to talking over the time I was up near Broome. It's where you come from, isn't it?'

'Yes,' Jackamara agrees, suddenly aware that without even meaning to he has stumbled onto the person who might be the ringleader of the racket, and the source of the printed material from the jail. Still, he can't work out the man's interest in the north and as he hasn't been there, he'll have to be on guard.

He smiles good-naturedly as Dick brings him tea. Their eyes lock. The young bloke has sniffed out the copper beneath the prison soap smell. He looks away, Dick sneers in triumph. Jackamara sips his tea, his eyes move over and about the library. He is on the job, searching for contraband and clues. The fat man engages him in conversation. He is interested in the tracking skills of the Aborigines and the tribe living on a particular cattle station. Jackamara gives him a name, then tells him that they are not his people. He talks about them, finding people and incidents from his own mission. The man is most interested. He files the information away. Some day it might come in handy . . .

Stamping of feet, rattling of landings, shouting of orders, the jangling of keys, and it is time to be locked in his cell. It is very small and has only room enough for a bunk and water and shit bucket. He lies down and goes over the details of the day, staring up at the window and the squares of metal. If he is correct, he already knows how egress and ingress is obtained from and into the prison; but why it should be happening is the mystery he must solve.

He tries to formulate plans, wondering how he can conduct

an investigation within the prison. Without freedom of movement he will be seriously handicapped. Well, he'll just have to see what the morrow will bring, and just then an eye appears at the peephole and the light is switched off. Jackamara lies there listening to the sound of the warders' boots going along the landing, and the steady click, click, click of light switches. He gets to his feet and goes to the door and peers out. The cell is wedged in a corner on the ground floor and the peephole commands a view of a large arc of the area. He is moving to angle his vision when the last of the lights is switched off and the stairs shake under the impact of two heavy pairs of boots crashing down on the metal steps. He finds the correct angle to have the foot of the stairs in view. The two warders reach the bottom and go towards the office. It is then that the bell peals at the block door. Jackamara swings his eye around. One of the warders goes to the door and opens it. Another warder enters and the other leaves. The man goes to the office, and then comes out to walk over to the side on which Jackamara's cell is and thus out of his field of vision. He listens. There is a sound of a key twisting in a lock, without the preceding jangling of key against key. Voices murmur. He has entered a cell and must be talking to an inmate. The murmur goes on for some time; but he cannot catch a word.

Finally, there is the sound of the cell door being locked and the warder walks into his arc of vision. This warder is let out from the block by the warder on night duty who then re-enters his office. Nothing more, except for a few lights being switched off later on. Jackamara lies on his bed, letting his mind wander into feeling. He has been in some difficult and awesome places in his life, but perhaps this is one of the worst. Here he is, penned up like an animal and can do nothing about it. Still, it is his duty, and the case does have interesting aspects. Why is the man interested so much in Broome? Now that is a puzzle, a piece which seems not to fit this particular case. Well, it has served a purpose, has given him an in and that is enough. Unable to sleep he gets up and tries to see out of the window. It is above his head and the sill is steeply sloping so that it is difficult to reach the bars. He leaps up, grabs the bars and pulls himself up. He looks out and directly up into a guard box. The white face of the guard is peering down towards the windows. And now comes the shout: 'Get down from that window!' Jackamara relaxes his grip and lets himself come back down on the floor. It feels only early and what can he do if he doesn't feel like sleeping. There isn't even enough room to pace up and down. He slumps down upon the bed, then gets up. A week is all, but is the week counted from today, or from tomorrow? Is it six days, or seven full days? He doesn't know, and he hasn't got much to think about either. Well, what will the morrow bring?

Jackamara turns on his side and the next thing it is morning and the warder is flinging open the door with a crash.

4

The Games Afoot

Jackamara pushes a broom along a landing, down the metal stairs and across the ground floor of the prison block. He comes to the only open door and peers through. A group of convicts sit at a long table at the head of which sits a grey man in civilian clothing who must be the welfare officer. Leaning on his broom, Jackamara plays the menial black man with a sort of dopey look on his face and hopes that it will come off if the warder comes to check why he is just standing there.

Puffs of smoke rise. The dozen convicts are smoking tailor-made cigarettes, obviously passed around by the civilian. Jackamara sees a carton of cigarettes in front of the fat librarian who sits to the right of the welfare officer. Next to him is the man who challenged him the day before and beside him is the librarian's cell-mate, an Aborigine or Nyoongah, and thus possibly a source of information. Jackamara has decided over just one day that a dangerous gang is controlling all that is illegal and legal in the cell block, and possibly in the entire prison. He also suspects that there is a network extending out through the warders into the port and possibly to the rest of the state. This last part is mere supposition, based on the fat man's interest in Broome, and there in the wall of the room where the convicts are exposing their problems to the welfare officer, is the door leading to the outside . . . This he must examine.

He hangs around, pushing the broom and waiting for the welfare business to be over. At last the convicts come out and the warder leaves his office to cluster them at the door leading into the main division. The welfare officer stands with them apparently at ease. While this waiting is continuing, Jackamara darts into the room and goes to the door. He is bent examining the hinges when a hand drops on his shoulder. He straightens up and meets the cold eyes of the librarian's assistant.

'What're you doing at that door?' the man grates, his eyes boring into those of the black man.

'Came in to clean and that door caught my eye. Thought maybe I could get a glimpse of the outside through the keyhole.'

'And what did you see?'

'Nothing, just plain nothing,' and Jackamara runs his broom over the surface of the table bringing down cigarette ash and dust. He goes to the end of the room and begins sweeping. The young bloke eyes him and then leaves . . .

It's 11.30 am and it's out to the main yard for a half-hour while all the work crews are coming in, and at midday it's lock-up time for dinner until 1.00 pm, and then work again. Jackamara and the other cleaners, with the librarian and Dick, pass through the doors, going from one screw to the other. They then must wait until he locks the door before they are escorted to the main yard gate, where they wait until he unlocks it, then pass through into the main exercise yard.

Jackamara decides to keep moving to keep away from the young bloke and to avoid having to talk to Robbi Singh about the north. Others are walking up and down the length of the yard. He follows their example, going slowly so that he can look around and pick his mark. He knows the bloke he wants to get to, and as he walks down the yard, he looks for him, and as he turns to go back up the yard, he breaks off and drifts in the direction of the young black bloke who was in with the welfare officer and who shares Robbi Singh's cell.

The young bloke is sitting next to Robbi Singh and the dangerous Dick is on the other side. It is not the best opportunity to say a 'hello' and he hesitates; but then the librarian sees him and beckons him over with one fat, crooked finger. His assistant scowls, but says nothing.

Jackamara comes and sits down near but not too near the fat bloke. Robbi Singh reaches into a pocket, pulls out a pack of tailor-mades, and tosses him one, then one to Dick and the young Aborigine. Jackamara has matches in his pocket and he pulls out the box and makes the mistake of passing it over to the young convict. The Nyoongah lights his own cigarette then the others from one match and pockets the box. Jackamara accepts this at first. He doesn't want to make a fuss, though not making one might make others see him as an easy mark. Well, let them. A week was only a week. He reconsiders his acquiescence, decides to make it an opening and snarls: 'The matchbox, kid.'

The young bloke looks across at him daring him to make a move. Well, this is it. He casually reaches across and takes the box of matches out of the kid's pocket and when the kid goes to snatch them back, Jackamara says: 'Eh, don't I know your uncle, what 'is name?'

This is an approved opening in a conversation with Aborigines. It sets the kinship lines stretching out and must be answered. 'You mean old Uncle Wally. He's down Brookton way, last time I heard.'

'That was after his operation?'

'What operation, he never had a sick day in his life.'

'Well, that must've been that Willy Morrison. Something to do with his lungs.'

'Yeah, that's right,' replies the young Nyoongah relaxing. 'You just got in. How's the outside?'

'Still there and sparking sometimes. Good get-together the other night at Midlands. Boy, I put away some piss. You been out there when you were roaming fancy-free?'

'I'm a Nyoongah, ain't I?'

'Dunno about that, you mixing with these'uns here. I was thinking of getting a transfer to Second Division where we all are.'

'Anyone from that tribe up north?' Robbi Singh suddenly enquires.

'Could be, but I'm here and not there. If I could get there I could check it for you.'

'Don't need you, I can do that,' the young Nyoongah exclaims.

'Yeah, you could, excepting you don't know those blokes,' Jackamara retorts. 'Besides you like it here.'

'Well, you can do it, smart arse. Anyway, I do like it here. Got good mates. Besides got more than enough time to change over, if I want to. There's a few Nyoongahs in this yard anyway. See, there's old Jimmy Mailer. He's the one that found that white lady drowned and washed up on the beach and slipped one into her. Got life for it; that means fifteen years, but I've got ten years and the key. I've got to earn my way out. Not like him. He can just cruise on from day to day. Fifteen years, bang, he's out. Me, ten years, then who knows? So, if I mix with the Nyoongahs, maybe they just forget about me. You know, they can throw away that key. "He seems pretty settled here, why not leave him here for another spell. He hasn't shown any signs of rehabilitation." That's how they talk and think. So, I have to look after myself. And then you with the Nyoongahs and some of the blokes get upset. They hear their woman's playing up on them, or one of their family dies, and it gets to them, and before you know it, the bloke's hammering out and there's a big fight on. I can't afford that, can't afford that at all. I wanta get out and to get out, I have to keep outa trouble, do those ten years, then the committee meets and I go before them, I haveta have something to show them. And I'm going to have something. Yeah.'

Jackamara opens his mouth to reply and it is dinnertime and the warders are flinging open the gates and ordering the men inside to line up. The New Block men are marched off to their division and as they pass through the gate they are given their dinner. A dixie containing soup on the bottom, and meat and two vegetables on the top. They take the warm dixies, then must stand outside and wait to be locked in. By that time their meals are cold, and when Jackamara opens the bottom of the dixie he sees that the soup has lumps of grease floating on top. Still, he is hungry enough to drink it down and during the course of his adventurous life, he has had worse. He then eats the rest of his dinner while he ponders his next move. Things are going smoothly and by the time the week is up, he should have a good idea of what is happening inside, and how it is linked up with The Panopticon Prison Reform Society!

Like a lot of the other cons in New Block, the young Nyoongah, Wildcat, as he calls himself, is reserved and suspicious of new prisoners. Jackamara finds it difficult to pump him; but as both are Aborigines, this gives them a certain bonding. Wildcat listens to him and laughs at his claims of innocence and his hopes to be out soon.

'Yeah, man,' he retorts. 'A lot of youse say that and in five years' time you'll still be in here with me. Doesn't matter if you're innocent or not. Well, I ain't innocent. Never been innocent. Guilty since the day I was born with this skin which marked me out.'

'Well, our skin colour is a mark of honour,' Jackamara says. 'It's great for the climate and you can't be seen in the dark.'

'Yeah, yeah, but what did it do for me, or what did I do for it? Do you know any of the old songs? Know one. Uncle Wally, well he taught it to me. Explained it too, but what did it mean to me? Nothing, that's what. Naw, in here, the only thing that has meaning is the walls. I'm fucked, uncle, into ten years and the key and there's no looking ahead for me.'

'Maybe,' Jackamara hints, and changes the subject from what are purely Aboriginal and personal concerns to the librarian. 'That librarian, Robbi Singh, how do you like sharing a cell with that much of a man? He's big that one is.'

'Big in more ways than body, you know. When I came

in with that sentence hanging over me, all that I felt like
was suicide. How could I do it? Well, he was there and
he got me together, just as he got himself together to do
his time. He doesn't let things get him down, not often
that is, and if they do, he's up and plotting again in no
time flat. A bloke in a million, he is.'

'Plottin' what?'

'Well, I mean, you know, things. Just that . . .' And
Wildcat begins whispering so that the other cons in the yard
where the conversation is taking place won't overhear. 'I
could tell you plenty about him. He's been in the army too.
The Chief Warder was his commanding officer, or something
like that. They were behind the lines in Malaya for a long
time, and . . .'

He goes silent as Dick comes drifting supposedly to cadge
a smoke. Jackamara looks down the yard waiting for him
to leave, but he slumps down beside them. His eyes lock
onto Jackamara. The bloke is ready to pick a fight. The
detective readies himself. You don't back down in boob;
Dick is saved by the bell. Time to be locked up for the
night . . .

Whenever possible, Jackamara cultivates Wildcat; but
Singh's assistant has him under surveillance and often puts
a stop in their conversation by his presence. The detective
finds Wildcat a babbler. It is as if he has been just waiting
for a chance to open up to someone, and now thinks he
has found that someone. He wanders about in words and
sentences, verbalising this and that, and into the stream of
words Jackamara skilfully inserts his questions. He learns
a little, though nothing about the fat man's interest in
Broome, but might have learnt something, except for Dick.
Jackamara is certain too that Wildcat doesn't know all that
much, for a man as experienced in deviousness as Robbi
Singh is unlikely to confide in a young inmate; but during
those long nights in the cell, he must have let things slip,
and it is a matter of ferreting these out. What Jackamara
feels he needs, is the time and place for a first-class

interrogation during which he can scrape the barrel of information clean; but it is impossible, and he has to listen to a lot of words which make him pity the kid. With only a few days of his week left, Jackamara can easily find pity for the kid with such an arid future stretching ahead. He also has found out that he is in only for pointing a gun at a copper and accidently discharging it. But under the law it is a heinous crime. A police constable has been shot and not only that but by a black man, and Jackamara knows this has caused the shit to hit the fan and splatter all over the kid. He has to be made an example, or else, at least according to this line of reasoning, next thing you'll have half the Western Australian Aboriginal population taking pot shots at police. The kid has been slung inside as an example, and for so long that when he gets out, he'll be completely institutionalised and a crim for all his miserable life. Jackamara has come in contact with such blokes and knows what he is thinking about. He likes the young Nyoongah and tries to help him by advising him to fill up his days with as many things as might help him to survive. One was getting an education. He is surprised (or rather not seeing that the kid has a brain in him) that he is already doing that, and this brings him back to the arch villain, Robbi Singh, for he has taken the kid under his crow's wing and has advised him to do so. So away with pity and back to his job. Singh is an out and out villain, as corrupt and conniving as they come, and what chance has the kid caught between the hammer of the law and the anvil of crime . . . ?

The ordered days march to Saturday and Jackamara gets his tobacco ration with the other cons and enters the main yard. He is standing there deciding on what he might do. An idea he considers is attaching himself to groups of cons talking about old jobs and picking up information that way, though as he isn't a West Aussie copper, he has little use for such random information. Still, some of the blokes are Queenslanders and maybe on the run. He is moving towards a group who are playing poker for matches, when a bloke comes up to him and says 'You wanta get into this game? Win more tobacco than you can smoke in a month of Sundays?'

Detective Watson Holmes Jackamara gives the little bloke who appears natty in the drab prison garb a hard cop look which is the same as a hard con look. He recognises a confidence trickster; but, interested to know any new lurks going down, he agrees. He is handing over half of his tobacco ration, when Wildcat comes over to warn him.

'It's on the up and up,' he tells him. 'You can win, but you have to get in ahead of all the other blokes and that's where the catch is.'

'Well, I can be lucky, can't I?'

'You'll crash out, that's what'll happen. You don't know anyone in the yard, and so when you have to get blokes to fill up the pyramid, you won't be able to.'

'I'll just see,' Jackamara replies, and gets into the game. He rises to be one of the two in the very next game and is to head his own pyramid. Now comes the problem. He can't recruit a single bloke. Most of them have been suckered before. The game collapses and when Jackamara goes to claim his tobacco back, he finds that he has lost it.

'See, I told you,' Wildcat says. 'If you want to win, wait a few weeks and start your own game, then you'll get out first.'

Jackamara nods, but he's remembering the diagram on the sheet of paper in the file and mention of the game which is spreading through Fremantle and Perth. The Commissioner seemed not to have been overly concerned about it; but Jackamara is. It is similar to the con game in which he has just lost his tobacco. So another link between inside and outside has been found. Detective Watson Holmes Jackamara smiles for the case is beginning to catch his interest. If only he could link up the north with it . . .

On Sunday, Jackamara goes to church to fill in the morning. His incarceration is beginning to drag and he feels that a straight investigation would be enough to uncover the scam.

He feels that he has learnt all that he can inside the prison, though there is one thing he would like to do before leaving. He hopes that he will have time and opportunity, though it must be done on a workday.

Monday morning, his seventh day and he is prepared to be taken across to the centre through which he passed into prison. But things remain as they were and are and will be and he begins his work, sweeping the landing, while wondering if he'll get out today and put the prison behind him. He comes down to the bottom of the stairs and finds himself alone. The warder is in his office; Robbi Singh and Dick either in the library, or collecting books somewhere, and the other cleaners are on the landings. This is his chance and he goes to Singh's cell door, takes out the wire key which Wildcat made and hides in a crack in the floor. He thrusts it into the big keyhole and turns it. The lock clunks back. He slips into the cell and pushes the door to.

Inside, his attention is drawn to the locker with the padlock on it. Even he, a new inmate is aware that a convict having a locked locker is a rare breed of animal, extinct if it ever existed. He goes to it and sees that it is a combination lock. Simple enough for one of his ability. His sensitive fingers move across the numbers. The padlock falls open. He pulls open the door. Chocolate, cigarettes, jam, tobacco, matches and in the bottom portion two thick ledgers and envelopes and paper. He opens one of the ledgers and sees that it is a list of names with amounts next to them. He flips on and there are diagrams filled in with names. The diagrams model the pyramid game he played on Saturday. Quickly, he copies down some of the names and addresses; then checks the other ledger which he finds are the accounts of The Panopticon Prison Reform Society. He is suprised to find that the society has funds of over 50 000 pounds. He notes this down, then thrusts the paper into his pocket. Before leaving the cell, he looks through the peephole. All clear. He is through the door, and a hand grabs his arm.

'Knew it,' a voice says triumphantly. 'Thought you were

more than you appeared. What were you doing in Robbi's cell, eh? Come on, let's go into the library.'

It is then that the doorbell jangles and the warder comes out of his office and opens the door. He listens, then looks back at the two. 'Arh, you Watson, you're wanted at the Admin Block. Seems like there's been a bit of a mix-up and you're being released.'

5

Filed

Detective Watson Holmes Jackamara is relieved to escape the prison. Doing time has made him think about making people do time. *Putting some villains inside,* he ponders, *might be justified; but others such as Wildcat?* He decides that they might be better off away from cities and temptations, and this causes him to consider Singh's connection with the north. Should he go into it, or not? He decides not to. If the investigation is pursued it might be gone into; but it will not be his job. He spends a day compiling his report, and the next morning takes the neatly typed pages along to the Commissioner. He has made an appointment for ten o'clock.

The Commissioner, as befitting his top of the rung position, has a female secretary. She stares at Jackamara as he enters the outer office. She was away on leave when Jackamara was there a week ago, and now wonders what an Aborigine is doing in the Commissioner's office, especially when there is not even a black constable on the Western Australian Police Force. Frowning, she places the problem in the too-hard basket, and lets the Aborigine wait until she finishes typing an affirmative answer to an invitation inviting the Commissioner to a special function of The Panopticon Prison Reform Society. She wonders briefly what it is, dismisses the thought and raises her head to stare at the Aborigine who waits patiently at her desk.

'Well?' she asks, drawing out the word.

Detective Jackamara gives her a cold look which makes her flush not with embarrassment, but with anger.

123

'I haven't got all day,' she snaps, looking down at the letter and noticing that she has spelt 'Panopticon' wrong. Drat, all his fault for towering over her while she typed. She glares up at him and her glare falls into the coldness of his eyes.

'Look, miss,' Detective Jackamara drawls, 'I had a ten o'clock appointment with the Commissioner. It now is ten minutes past ten. I suggest that you let him know that I have arrived. Detective Watson Holmes Jackamara of the Queensland Police.'

'Oh,' she replies, and with her heels tapping angrily she quickly goes to the door and knocks on it.

Jackamara hears her say that there is a black detective waiting to see him. He does not catch the reply. The woman sweeps back and points at the doorway. He goes into the office and closes the door behind him. Steely-grey eyes regard him, and a gesture bids him to approach and place the file on the desk. Jackamara does so and stands at attention while the grey head bends over the file. At last the head rises and the mouth opens to say: 'I see.'

The eyes regard the detective, who feels that he should say something: 'Simple enough case, sir. First of all I found the door through which they were entering and leaving the prison. The hinges had been oiled as had the padlock on the bar across the outside. Then the bottom of the door was level with the ground and scraped the sandstone when it was opened. From the marks I would say that the door has been opened and shut about twenty times over the last month, or so. I also verified this from the inside.'

'I see,' the Commissioner repeats, and Jackamara doggedly continues.

'It seems that a convicted murderer by the name of Robbi Singh is the brains behind what I see to be a confidence scheme of some ingenuity and cunning. Of course, I do not know the ramifications of the outside scheme; but everything goes through The Panopticon Prison Reform Society. If you refer to my report, you'll see examples of the names of people who have donated moneys to this, this organisation. Quite large sums too. You'll find lists of donors and the books of the society in Singh's cell. It should be a simple matter to retrieve them.'

'I see,' the Commissioner repeats again.

The detective doggedly continues: 'I have described a game of, of some ingenuity, I saw being played within the prison, the main exercise yard to be specific. I feel that a variant of this game has been exported outside.'

The Commissioner finally comments: 'I take it that the game is a confidence trick?'

'No, sir, not exactly. It is possible to win, if you enter the game at the beginning, but then very quickly the odds increase so steeply against you that it is impossible to get your tobacco back.'

'Tobacco?'

'Yes, sir, I played the game in the exercise yard of the prison.'

'Would you not say that it is a mild form of gambling?'

'Quite close to that, sir.'

'And illegal?'

'Perhaps, sir. I am not up on the gambling laws of this state.'

'Continue.'

'I would like to have it placed on record that the young man who shares the cell with Robbi Singh was most cooperative. It was he who passed over certain information that indicated that the Chief Warder has a close relationship with the convict, Robbi Singh. It seems that the ramifications of the swindle, and it appears to be that, are quite extensive and a thorough investigation should be made to tie up the loose ends. The first thing is to get those books from Singh. I have indicated their nature in my report and the necessity for quick decisive action.'

The Commissioner looks down at the report and idly flips through the papers; 'A commendable job, if I may say so, but I see no reason for follow-up action to be taken as yet.

Since your preliminary investigation, events have overtaken it, I'm afraid.'

'What events, sir? I feel that if prisoners can leave and enter the prison at will in collusion with corrupt penal officers, steps should be taken to put a stop to it.'

'Detective Jacky, Jackamara I feel that you misunderstood the nature of your assignment. Again much of what you have given me is mere supposition . . .'

'Mere supposition, but a follow-up investigation will flesh out the bones. It's only a matter of surveillance to catch them red-handed.'

'No, the investigation is over, and your report will go no further than this room. Yesterday, Mr Robbi Singh was given a full pardon and has now been released. He is a remarkable man, a most remarkable man . . .'

'Yes, but a dangerous one. Perhaps steps should be taken to deport him back to India. There is a matter of some interest that I have since learnt . . .'

'He is an Anglo-Indian, Detective Jackamara, and not only that but a war hero. Evidence came to light that the incident for which he was tried and found guilty was . . . well, no matter.'

'And the Chief Warder?'

'You could not be aware that the Superintendent of Fremantle Prison suffered a heart attack yesterday and the Chief Warder has taken his place. His reputation and knowledge of the penal system is second to none. The superintendent recommended him himself. He too, I must remind you, is a war hero. I must say that these, these allegations, if they got out, would be most detrimental not only to him, but to the Penal Department.'

'And the swindle?'

'A figment of your imagination. The Panopticon Prison Reform Society is above reproach. Some of Western Australia's foremost citizens are active in it. The Governor is a patron. I'm afraid that your report doesn't warrant a follow-up investigation. Of course, I'll see that an eye is kept on the society and on Mr Robbi Singh, and add your report to my personal files; but that is all.'

'And so my doing time was a waste of time?'

'No, no, not at all, we have to know what is going on. This is a small state and I, as Commissioner of Police, must be informed on what may or may not be instances of commission of crimes. Prevention is better than apprehension, and so, I thank you for adding to my knowledge of some of our foremost citizens as well as, well, shall we say of prison reform as set out in the Panopticon Society. Arrangements have been made for you to catch the evening flight back to Brisbane. I think that is all. A report of your behaviour shall be forwarded to the Queensland Police. The Commissioner is a good friend of mine. I assure you that he shall be most discrete, as I know you shall be. Your oath to secrecy in police operations is binding, as I need not tell you.'

Detective Watson Holmes Jackamara goes out and closes the door gently behind him. He stands there for a moment shaking his head. He can't understand it. Then the woman calls him over and gives him a ticket on that evening's TAA flight. He looks at it, shakes his head again, then decides to return to the prison as a detective to see if he can talk a little sense into Wildcat. The slight connection between Singh and the north enters his mind. Perhaps, yes, he might see Singh's file and find out a little more before he leaves Perth. It is from such slight indications that crimes emerge into the full light of day, he thinks as he leaves the office after catching a glimpse of the invitation for the Commissioner to attend a function of The Panopticon Prison Reform Society. An interesting case indeed; but he has been dealt out of it. He ruefully shakes his head. He has never been north and he has a spot of leave coming up. Should he, or shouldn't he? He'll sleep on it. After all it is a Western Australian matter and has nothing to do with him.

CONTINUANCE

1

Wildcat Dreaming

'I t was like this, see, a way of getting out of the country, see a bit of the world. Five bob a week tourists, they called us, or we called ourselves. Camped under those pyramids in Gyppoland. There they had us running and skipping, falling and crawling all across the desert, and, you know, it was all hot and sandy, like West Aussie. We often got to wondering just why we were there. We had joined up to give the poms a bit of a hand, have a go at the Hun, and here we were in Egypt. It was god-awful. And the Gyppos? "Hey, Aussie, you want drink, grog? I show you where." And the grog tasted like pee, just like boob home-brew; but it did the trick; and then there was the other thing: "You want girl, jiggy-jig?" You hear the one about the padre. He went to Cairo and was surrounded by these kids, little kids, and they chant: "Hey, Aussie, you want jiggy-jig?" And this holy Joe, he smiles at these kids, then turns to a digger and asks: "They like us, what does jiggy-jig mean?"

'And the jiggy-jig wasn't up to much either. We used to go to the Woozer, the street of the swinging tit, right near that Shepherd's Hotel where the officers used to take their tea, or chota pegs and be all la-di-dah. Well, the Woozer was like our Roe Street; but with more of the gash, and every night was Saturday night, that is if you had the pennies. We used to drink the bad plonk at a Greek place, get tanked up and stagger along shouting at the harlots, and if we had the wherewithal we'd dash in for a quickie. Wasn't all that great, but it stopped the hair growing on your palms. Lucky here, you get shaving gear, or most of you'd have palm hair touching the floor by now. Well, the Woozer and paying for this, and not much of it, got our goat. On our last leave, we decided to settle a few scores. There was this one house run by a Greek madam, all black hair and stained teeth and lard and with a private telephone to the MPs so that if a bloke tried to put his wick in without paying the toll, he came out to find that he'd be carrying a sandbag around the parade ground until he dropped. Well, that last night, we got stuck into the plonk at the Greeks, and when he demanded more money, we demanded his money and then put a match to his grog. The place went up with a whoosh and we all cheered, and we ran away and to that whorehouse.

'Reached there and piled in. There was the madam in her black silk and her hair all piled up and her black eyes flashing at the pennies she thought she'd get from us. We flung the Greek's money down her dress and called for the girls. They came down, sagging tits, bleached hair, poxed up and ugly as sin. We got into them and swapped around. The madam rent her garments, demanding more cash. All she got was us throwing the bed and mattresses out of the windows. We piled them up in the middle of the street and made ourselves a bonfire. Then the MPs came and we decided to do them. They fired a couple of shots in the air and began backing away. We came at them, and found ourselves near Shepherd's and in front of a line of pommy soldiers with fixed bayonets. That put the wind up us; but an officer came out and things quietened down. He knew us poor bastards were bound for the Cove next day . . .'

With Clarrie, his words keep coming and coming, and they're all about the same thing. Comfort in a way. They drone on. You've heard it all before and before you know it, you begin nodding off. I need that, for I'm in the shit. Dick says that that Johnny Watson was a copper and had come to spy on us. I dunno about that; but strange he was in for five years one day, and then gone the next. It never happens like that. Dick is right. Okay. He's right; but why doesn't he shut up about it! Have to take refuge in the silly old fart's words to escape him going on about me being a blabbermouth and trusting anyone who had a dark skin. Fuck it, how did I know that he was a cop!

I thought coppers came in flat feet and big boots, silver buckles all down the front and a cap and a badge and all that jazz. Well, man, was I sadly mistaken. They are like flies and come in all the shades of the rainbow of human deceit . . . Christ, I've fucked up and feeling mean. Want to take a swipe at that Dick. Would do it too; but he's due for release in a few days and that might put it back. Can't do it. There's Clarrie; but the old codger is too old. So I hit no one and just sit there feeling mean and bad. Things are going fine, then something happens and they explode all round; now nothing is happening, excepting for that screaming in my head, and the smug look Dick has for me. I think he doesn't like Nyoongahs that much; but one of us'uns a cop? It's too much! This Wildcat, he tries to fly . . . They won't let him; pull him down, nail him down on a cross like Jesus, and before he knows it, he's screaming in pain, suffering for all the times he's opened his mouth when he shouldn't have. The shit is raining down on me. I feel like I'm about to explode. My face snarls and my fists clench. I wanta get into a fight, get some action going; wanta stand tall; wanta put all this behind me; wanta show that fucker, and, you know, I can't show anyone at all. I'm stretched out on that cross extending over ten years and beyond, and only a committee, not a heavenly father, can take me from it. Yeah, they got that key, the claw hammer to jerk out the nails of my time, and if I step outa line, that cross is going to be eternally occupied. An eternity of boob; an eternity of eyes and being escorted here and there and back and forwards. Fuck it, too much for a body to stand. Ain't got any songs to sing; ain't got any fights to fight; I'm a loser, man. They've nailed me to my time, and if I even moan a little, ease a limb, it's on my report and a screw swings on my legs, or pokes a baton into my side and taunts me forever and a day. So, there's only the pain and I want, feel that I gotta do something, make it as big, as large, as tall as the walls surrounding me. Make it an eternity thing, then I won't have anything to lose and the screaming will go away, won't it, won't it? Thank God for Clarrie and his voice droning on, edging out that scream . . .

'None of you'll believe this, not one of you, but me, I was the last one outa the Cove. The last lighter was just pulling out from the shore, when I come out of that scrub hollering and shouting, and the sailor whose just untied the mooring rope sees me and I'm saved. The last one off, and you know how it happened. When they decide on the evacuation, they take us off little by little, in dribs and drabs; but don't bring in the perimeter. We hold on to our positions and just get thinner and thinner, fewer and fewer in the trenches. Getting into winter, near Christmas, different there it gets colder and colder about that time, and Jacko Turk, well, he didn't miss us. He was just trying to keep warm. Well, we are the last few blokes, have to stay in our positions till four or so in the morning. Nice quiet night and I decide me to have a kip. Tell the blokes, great cobbers they were, to wake me up when it's time, then went into the dugout for forty winks. I wake up. Silence all around, just a few guns firing in the distance. Christ, the trench is empty. They're pulled out and left me. Race down towards the beach. It's the silence, the emptiness that gets me. This place had been another home for me, like Freeo. No problems and you learn to live with the shells, the bullets, the cold steel. Now that home was no more. Feel a tear in my eye as I hurry through that scrub, down the track, and I swear, I tell you, from the corner of my eye I catch shadows moving, following along. Our dead cobbers trying to come along with the last live one there. They didn't make it. Cold, rotting in their graves; but I did and now I'm in Freeo, in the land of the living dead. Not much difference between there and here. It was like a boob sentence, nigh on twelve months . . .'

Christ, nothing like Clarrie to raise my spirits. I know that I'll be the last one from this place. When it closes man, when they evacuate this prison, I'll be carted away, all grey-haired and ancient. Fuck, no future, except these grey walls. The city of the lonesome dead, filled with ghosts and sad sights. How low can I get. Got the 'Down in the Gutter Blues' and the sound of Clarrie's voice is inciting me to violence when this message comes, when this escort comes and I go along with the screw, shambling along now a real convict, now feeling the blade of the knife of my despair, of my revenge, cool and sharp along my loins. Good feeling that. Easy to whip it out and sink it into the eternity of my time. Hurrah, for this here Wildcat. Now he's up for life. Well, it ain't more than I've got now. Vengeance calls in hot, hot pants, and I'm starting to float a little with the tension. I drift into that pokey little office in the admin block and that blade is feeling so good along my cock that I know I can make my point with it. Get it? You might, if you don't watch out. Careful, Wildcat, who done this to you? They all did. Nailed me on that cross and left me alone with my time streaming from me, like a slashed vein bleeding; bleeding, and I watch the blood spurting, staining my future red with this, this incarceration. Amen to that, and the Salvos sing 'The Old Rugged Cross' and Clarrie blabs on about the Anzacs landing, and the soldiers line up on both sides of my tribespeople. Great-grandfather sees them coming, and the blood spills all over the land, and men, women and children lie in the dust of my cell, and all their spirits call to me, and . . . So I enter into that pokey office and there's this copper waiting for my blade. He's not there to offer me a deal. Ain't no deals for a bloke with a future eating into ten years and after that the key. Don't want that future; just want it to be this present present with the feeling of that blade digging into the front of my hip. Why that copper want to see me anyway? Can one add time onto eternity? What am I supposed to say to him, or he to me? I slump into a chair opposite him, stare at the rough surface of the table and let my blues wash over me:

> Trouble in mind, trouble in mind,
> But I won't be blue always,
> The sunshine's going to shine,
> Through my arsehole some day.

So there he is in front of me. His black face gleaming and teeth gleaming in a smile. Is he sincere? Christ, it's like something else; it's like I was some place else. Some place I can feel about; somebody I can puzzle about. There was this woman I used to watch. White woman, blonde hair, blue-eyed. She used to sit on the steps of her house most days. I wondered about her, wondering why she sat on those steps. There wasn't anything there worth seeing, and nothing doing on the street. Just the traffic chuffing past, and me watching her through the curtains of my room, a room like a cell excepting no bars on the window. I'm a great one for rooms. Get one and sit and drink a bottle of port or sherry, just watching the world go past in a hurry. Yeah, everyone in a hurry excepting me: no job, no future, just a Beckett character. I must go on; I will go on, somehow. No future anyways. Christ, ten years and more in one place, eyes watching you do your time. No need to hurry, boy, because this is your life, not nice in grammar and all, which gets me to thinking about the book that I'm writing and how they, the welfare officer, the grey mouse, and the teacher, the brown rabbit, not the skin, eh, the suit. They tell me to watch my grammar and make it right, even though I'm more concerned about the subject matter. Learning all the time during my time, knowing all those words, because I read that encyclopedia. Yeah, I'm a well-read man, or what have you, and this bloke is waiting to interview me. Well, I've got the answer to all his questions: a cool blade.

I sit opposite him and feel betrayed. How could one of us'uns become a cop, and worse than that, a demon, a detective, and one who came to spy on us, on me? A con a few days ago, now free and a copper, just like the one I shot, though he was in uniform. Well, I play it cool, I sit nice and easy and smile as I feel the pressure of that blade. He looks back at me, outa those big brown eyes of his and I'm seeing black not a copper, but that is what they are like. Get your confidence and before you know your big mouth is flapping and those gates are agaping wide for you.

'Hi,' I say, 'didja like the yard? Last time I saw you you were one of us.'

'Yeah,' he replies, and his 'yeah' lies down in front of me like a corpse.

'What did they get you for this time?' I ask, making with the joke though it's not very funny. This bloke has an out as well as an in, and when he was in, he always had an out. Me, man, I've only got an in.

'Well, it's like this. You boy, ain't going very far for the future and the far future. It's sad how you young'uns end up.'

'I know that,' I say back to him quick smart, hiding any agitation I feel, just as I'm hiding the shiv in my pants.

'I'm going back to my own state,' he says, then adds. 'It's pretty fucked up here. Not my country at all, though I hear the north is nice . . .'

'What do you mean?' I ask.

'Well, once they get on top, that's where they stay, no matter what any of us can do. They run the business and we have to go along with it.'

'Suppose so, never bothered me none, I knew it from the day I was born. My mum knew, my uncle, my grandfather and best of all my great-grandfather. He was there when they murdered us. They called it the battle of Pinjarra; but "battle" should be spelt "m-a-s-s-a-c-r-e".'

'Yeah, they did it everywhere. Now a lot of us end up like you have. You fight, you lose, they win. Maybe we should rethink our tactics.'

'I surely would, if I could,' I sneer at him. 'My big problem is getting out of here.'

'I tried to put in a good word for you . . .'

'Yeah, bully for you; but I don't believe in fairy tales no how. My uncle, he's a bit like you, though he don't go after people. He catches and skins those rabbits. Gets a bob or so for the skins, but he's not part of much, not like you, like me. We's all Beckett characters shuffling through life. One sad foot after the other. You catch people and put them inside. I get caught and end up inside. That's life. Catching and being caught.'

'Who's this Beckett?' he asks.

'Just a loser like me. He writes books about losers too.'

'You ain't no loser,' he replies, and I have to think about that, for being in boob for ten years and after that the key. Well, if I ain't a loser, show me someone who is.

'All right for you saying that,' I shrug, 'you're out there and I'm in here.'

'But one day, you'll be out here, so you have to think about it,' he comes back at me.

'Yeah,' I say, thinking about the beginning of my book and what I had written about being released. It was scary after nine months, it'll be much worse after the long stretch I'm doing now. How can I handle it?

'I know people like you, and what you become,' he says. 'You make this place a home and can't handle freedom any more. If you let it get to you, you'll settle in here and bang goes your life.'

I don't like how the conversation is going, and he don't know shit. Ain't I writing that book to earn some good points? Ain't I keeping out of trouble? I ain't happy in here. Don't know how I can be. Robbi got out just the other day and there's a great hole where he used to be, and I want to fill that hole with having a go at the blokes who've been putting me down. Dick for one, but he's getting out in a couple of days too, and that'll be another hole. It's easy to give him a good thumping when the screws are outa the way; but the others. They're taking the opportunity to start snarling and picking. Bully for them, Wildcat knows how to spit and claw in return, but he can't. He wants out, and they know this, know that any brawls I get into are going to be against me when that time comes to go up before the board. Cons, fuck, they're all the same. One for one, and never all for all.

'So,' he says, 'I just wanted to say hang on and then after you get out, look me up. I'll be home in Queensland and still on the force, because I haven't any other place to be either.' Then he smiles as he adds: 'After all I've been inside and know what it's like.'

I smile back, and reply: 'I wanted to make it to the east that time. That's why I'm in here now. I'll look you up, man, just march into Police Headquarters in Brisbane and say I'm looking for you. Fine,' and I grin sardonically.

And that's it. Interview terminated, except something about him being back this way again and coming to see me; and then something about the north and Robbi being interested in it. I smirk and say something about maybe he has bought a goldmine up there. He looks interested and I laugh it away. I'm keeping my mouth shut this time. We shake hands, just imagine that, shaking hands with a detective; but if Robbi can have his Chief Screw, why can't I have a demon? Then I'm escorted back feeling a bit better because I know that he is one of us. Just like a Nyoongah playing his cards close to his chest, giving me a wink and a nod, and 'see you one year' which leaves me with a smile. It's only as I'm going back to the division that I feel that blade. I'm glad that I didn't use it. Must finish my book now and see what happens. Still, I've got an empty cell to be locked up in. No more, Robbi, perhaps for ever . . . But then from him I've learnt that everything comes in shades of grey. He's taken my innocence along with him and left me with the will to survive. I don't know if I like this, or not. When I was young things seemed easier and harder at the same time. Fuck it, more shades of grey. You know, I'm tired of thinking. It's painful. Just want to be. Even the scream in my head is better than uncertainty.

2

Coping

Sharing a cell with Robbi Singh helped me along the way—what with his teaching me to concentrate my mind on the space between my eyebrows—and so did that interview with the demon, Watson Holmes Jackamara. When Robbi got his things together and was escorted outa my life, he took some light along with him. The screaming began in my mind, then that black demon came along and sorta treated me like a human being. You know, I got back some hope and the screaming went away. I came back to the cell and it was quiet and not that empty. Robbi used to fill it with his bulk. Now all I've got is myself and my books and papers. I can do some work and even, don't laugh, start to prepare for the time when I'm out of here. Things aren't too bad. The Panopticon Prison Reform Society has been taken outside with Robbi and there'll be no more friendly visits from the screws. But as Robbi thought up a scam to fill his time, I set my mind to thinking too. Have to find something to fill my time, give it meaning and gain some points. I'm at the mercy of others; but I'll never give in to them, you dig!

And I've got this new job now too. Prison librarian and that means I've got access to all the books. There's my row of Beckett, and I begin to check over his style; though I'm beginning to think I need someone with a bit more hope. Life isn't all just a matter of going on. I have to get my finger out and so what if I've got about five years remaining and after that I've got to front the board which will judge the first ten years. Have to be nice and bear each and everything, put my consciousness between my eyebrows when things get too tough and blank out; but my book is finished and I can't just cruise along until that time when the gates will swing open to eject me free at last from this hell hole, but when it does, I just might go east and look up that demon. Surprise him. I get ten shillings a week here and I spend about half of that on toothpaste and things. After ten or so years it'll mount up enough to get me east. So things aren't all that bad. Naw, I can make it, if I find something to fill in all that time. Push that scream away and fall into good thoughts. I finished that book, didn't I? Yes, I did.

Night time in my lonely cell, if you can call it lonely, what with the screw's eye looking through the peephole and the mutterings of the cons all around me, I lie in my bunk and look at the light shining through the window grille, and strangely, the full moon becomes framed there. I stare at it. I want to fly . . .

Old Crow comes to squawk to me. 'You want to fly?' he says, and I see the gloating look in his eye and I know that he ain't going to teach me anything. I reply, 'Yeah,' and rise towards the moon. I pass through the grille and laugh as I soar high and away from Crow. The night sky is a silver dish. I move under it. I feel the stars beam through my body. I'm as light as feathers, as insubstantial as moonbeams. I exult in my freedom. I leave the barren city behind me and reach the dark thoughtfulness of the bush. I swoop down and alight in Uncle Wally's camp. He sits there muttering a song in the old language. I stand there listening awhile, then he says: 'Sit down, boy.'

I sit at the fire watching the flames flickering, feeling the shadows stir around me, feeling the stars and the moon passing through me. 'How are you, boy?' he says. 'Long time no see.'

'Yeah, I'm in that big house in Freeo,' I reply.

'Arrh, you there? Your grandaddy was on Rottnest. You following in his footsteps? Nothing better than the bush though.'

'Yeah, peaceful,' I say.

'It lives in you,' he says. 'It calls you, if you let it.' And he begins singing that song he sang to me a long time ago. I know that I know it, and sing back the verses.

'Lots of things they can't take away from us,' he says. 'Lots of things they don't know about.'

And then he goes quiet and we sit along that fire and a sense of freedom comes over me. Suddenly, for the first time in a long spell, I feel happy. Absurd, but I am. Now I know that I can make it, and that no one can break me. I have something special in me which can't be touched, which has its own freedom. They can lock up my body; they have thrown away the key, but if I let it, my spirit can roam free. And as I look across at my old uncle, I get an idea to add to my points. I'm going to make it, and to make it I have to show that I'm reformed. More so I have to fill in my time, and there is a lot of us in jail, and I've written this book and know how to put words together. Then there's having been with Robbi and thus having an in to the screws, the grey mouse and the brown rabbit. I'll talk to them, see if I can get a Nyoongah group together, teach them English, or writing, or something like that. Different from what Robbi did, but it'll give me points and I won't be all alone, and, and . . . I'll do it. Man, I can fly, and perhaps, perhaps I can teach others to fly. I look across at old Wally and he smiles and I smile. We'll win through, all of us.

THE END

THE MASTER OF THE GHOST DREAMING
MUDROOROO

Lost is the way to the skyland. Our souls wander forlornly in the land of the ghosts. Our spirits become their play things; our bodies their food, to be ripped apart, and our gnawed bones are scattered. We are in despair; we are sickening unto death; we call to be healed. Anxiously we wait for our mapan, *the Master of the Ghost Dreaming to deliver us.*

In the first years of the nineteenth century, a small Aboriginal tribe reels under the threat of white invasion of their ancestral lands. Fada, a missionary from London, is attempting to impose a Christian God over their ancient beliefs. Fada and his wife Mada bring with them disease and despair, along with a message of hope — the result of their own Cockney dreaming.

This novel by Mudrooroo (formerly Colin Johnson), author of *Wild Cat Falling*, is a story of survival — physical, metaphysical and magical. It is also the story of Jangamuttuk, the custodian of the Ghost Dreaming, and his shamanistic efforts to will his tribe back to its own promised land.

STRADBROKE DREAMTIME
OODGEROO NUNUKUL

Years ago, my family — my Aboriginal family — lived on Stradbroke Island. Years before the greedy mineral seekers came to scar the landscape and break the back of this lovely island. I recall how we used to make the trip to Point Lookout. My father would saddle our horses at early light and we would make our way along the shoreline, then cut inland to climb over the hills covered with flowering pines, wattles and gums. The brumbies would watch our approach from a safe distance. These wild horses never trusted man, their foe. They would nuzzle their foals, warning them to stay away from their enemy.

Kath Walker (Oodgeroo Nunukul) spent her childhood with her family on Stradbroke Island, off the Queensland coast. The first half of this book, 'Stories from Stradbroke', describes episodes from her childhood days — some happy, some sad — and gives a memorable impression of Aboriginal life on the island and of a family proud of its Aboriginal heritage. The second part of the book, 'Stories from the Old and New Dreamtime', is made up of Aboriginal folklore which the author recalls hearing as a child, and of new stories written in traditional Aboriginal forms.

'Always vigorous, and deeply committed.'
OXFORD COMPANION TO AUSTRALIAN LITERATURE